Kissing the Cheek of Time

Laurie Brady

Kissing the Cheek of Time

Kissing the Cheek of Time
ISBN 978 1 76109 492 7
Copyright © text Laurie Brady 2023
Cover image: Cotton Bro Studio from Pexels

First published 2023 by
Ginninderra Press
PO Box 3461 Port Adelaide 5015
www.ginninderrapress.com.au

'Death not merely ends life, it also bestows upon it a silent
completeness, snatched from the hazardous flux to which
all things human are subject.'
– *The Life of the Mind*, Hannah Arendt (1975)

Peter

He'd remember the detail. At times like these, most people's senses are dulled. His were fine-tuned, more acute than normal. This was true of a close friend's death all those years ago, and his unusual awareness of the rural hospital's textured brick, the lawn, the scent of the would-be cheerful flowers in the front garden, and the picture of the arthritic elms flexing with timeless unconcern in the winter chill.

But why think of death? A bit ghoulish, he thought with a hint of a smile as he entered Mr Enright's waiting room – specialists apparently preferred Mister to Doctor. If there was threat, and he thought that unlikely, it was yet to be realised. Still, you could never be sure.

The décor was the era's salmon-pink and grey. A long armless lounge in charcoal fabric sat against one wall. Black plastic chairs occupied other spaces, fortunately nothing in blood-red. A Renoir print of *Luncheon of the Boating Party* hung above the lounge, and a small coffee table held a vase of tenth-real flannel flowers, and scattered magazines.

A large rectangular fish tank, lit to a luminous pale blue, probably to calm the nerves of patients, filled the only other empty space. If a patient's first impression of a waiting room gave the fertile imagination a feeling about the news they might receive, he was none the wiser. Basic or functional were the words that came to mind.

He approached the receptionist, who sat behind a chest-high counter of teak, an attractive, fortyish woman with a tangle of carroty red hair. She asked his name with a warm smile, and gave him a form on a clipboard to complete. That done, he returned to his seat and watched the rounded mouthing of the golden fish that glided with goitred eyes among the swaying ferns in their silent fluorescent world, and felt that his own life was a little like theirs.

He began to imitate the rounded mouthings of the fish, stopping when he noticed the receptionist watching him and smiling broadly. He was embarrassed but grateful, and returned her smile. It was a connection of sorts. At a time like this, it was relationship he wanted.

A middle-aged woman with protuberant eyes sat opposite him on the lounge, her face scourged to a would-be rosy health, and with a khaki envelope of unopened scans on her lap. He tried to make eye contact, feeling a confederacy of sorts.

'Are you OK?' he asked the woman, surprised that it was his voice they both heard. It sounded as if it emerged from the depths of the fish tank or from some other subterranean world.

She looked up, startled, and nodded with a barely heard 'Thanks', and lowered her eyes again. There was to be no comfort in sharing.

Ellie had wanted to come with him for moral support, because she could tell he was worried, but he'd downplayed its significance and said he'd prefer to go alone. He was wishing he hadn't. His annual blood test had revealed some anomalies.

'Look,' she'd said, waving the dictionary in her hand, '"anomaly, an aberration or irregularity, it's something that can't be easily explained".'

'Yes, but the GP thought it was worth sending me to this Enright, and why couldn't the results be easily explained?'

'Lots of things can't be explained, Peter. It's not a perfect science. Remember how my blood pressure was sky high, then low, they couldn't explain that either.'

'Well, it's not the same thing,' he answered and, realising he was being irrational, he smiled. 'Of course you're right. It's probably nothing at all.'

'Then I can come with you?'

'No…really. You've convinced me. I'm fine. At sixty-seven, darling, these visits are likely to become more frequent for both of us. Things change, we start to wear out.'

'Speak for yourself. Look at this beautiful body,' and she pirouetted with panache. 'And I haven't noticed too much decline in you…if you know what I mean,' and she grinned.

They'd laughed, embraced, and he'd left feeling upbeat. But as he drove to the hospital, he was bothered by why he'd resisted Ellie coming. Was it just a case of downplaying its significance, or was it that he needed to deny his own vulnerability, to her and to himself. Machismo.

Conscious of being watched by the nervy woman with the scans, and by the receptionist who was waiting for another comic performance of fish imitations, he took the few steps to the coffee table, sifting through the magazines, scanning the covers with their lurid news of surprising liaisons, wild sex romps and unwanted pregnancies, but not finding one suitable to his tastes, returned to his seat and listened for sounds behind the door, beyond the wadded stillness of the waiting room. There were none.

After a few minutes, a door opened and closed. An old white-haired man with a doughy face and pallid eyes made difficult going of his retreat from the doctor's room, breathing heavily and banging his walking stick on the lino floor with each step. For Peter, it sounded like an ominous metronome beating time.

His eyes were drawn to the different people in the Renoir painting on the wall, and he found himself entering the life of each of them, the woman in the flowered hat sitting at the table petting her dog, the stern bearded man in his top hat, imagining their comings and goings, saddened by the stilled gaiety.

Several minutes passed. He stretched his legs, closed his eyes and drifted. When he opened them, he caught the eye of the receptionist. She coloured, smiled and turned away quickly.

'Peter Allthorpe.'

The door opened again, and the specious safety of uncertainty was gone.

Mr Enright was lean, younger than he'd expected, dressed in a navy suit and maroon tie, with intelligent, self-deprecating eyes, silvery temples, and a gentle manner that inspired immediate confidence. He motioned Peter to a leather swivel chair and moved from behind his desk, carrying Peter's referral and blood test report.

Peter relaxed. At least the desk would not be a barricade to protect the bearer of unwanted truths.

'I see there were some anomalies in the blood tests,' Enright said softly, and began to scan the report and letter of referral.

Peter watched the expression on his face, and couldn't read anything in it. 'Should I be worried?' he asked tentatively and feeling like a school boy who'd been sent to the principal's office expecting the worst. 'The other doctor, my GP, reckons it's not unusual, especially in older people,' he added, searching for confirmation.

'Well, let's not get ahead of ourselves,' Enright said calmly. 'But you're right. Sometimes things just settle down, symptoms change. Climb up there and take off your shirt, loosen your belt.'

Peter moved to a high padded bench overlaid with white paper towelling, removed his shirt and lay down.

'Are you comfortable?' Enright asked before he began to probe around his neck and abdomen with cold vanilla-smelling fingers.

Peter wanted to tell Enright about his regular exercising, a lifetime habit, and of his tennis, as if it might be a factor in eliminating medical problems. Brownie points as defence. Ego, he told himself, and it has nothing to do with what Enright is looking for. Looking for? Is it something he suspects?

'Any fatigue, loss of appetite and weight, any unusual night sweating, any swelling in the glands?'

Peter shook his head to each symptom. Enright continued probing gently.

'I do get more tired now,' he added light-heartedly with a lame attempt at humour, 'but I am in my late sixties. Otherwise no.' He said this more emphatically as if he needed to dismiss Enright's suspicions, but wasn't reassured by the doctor's surprise at his answers.

Peter finished dressing, and Enright motioned to the chair, washing his hands and returning to his desk.

'I'd like you to have an MRI scan.'

'Do you have some idea of what it might be, doctor…if anything?'

Peter asked, knowing he would not be told of any suspicions the doctor had.

'Can't really say yet. I mentioned anomalies before. It's better we be sure. The scan will give a clearer picture.'

The woman with the unopened envelope of scans, the only other patient, was looking even more anxious as Enright shook his hand at the door, and moved across to whisper to the receptionist to arrange the next appointment. Peter wondered if their talk needed to be subdued in the interests of patient sanity.

He drove home feeling nothing very much. Reason and anxiety had agreed to a truce. When asked later by Ellie what he had been thinking on the way home, he wasn't able to give a satisfactory answer, and settled for 'I don't think I was thinking of anything very much.'

His reverie was broken by Frank, his seventy-year-old neighbour as he climbed from the car. 'Deep in thought, mate. You were miles away. Are you all right?'

'Yes, I'm fine,' Peter answered, surprised.

Frank was always sitting on his veranda, where sunlight crystallised his memories, trapping them like flies in honey. He'd been living there alone long before Peter and Ellie had arrived in Epping. He was old and surly with roving eyes, and deep creases in his bronzed forehead and cheeks like knife cuts. His bitterness against the world would always turn to delight when humankind was found guilty of indifference or cruelty.

His house was the only weatherboard in the street, and the exterior, a white turned the colour of parchment with age, bubbling rather than flaking, hadn't been painted for decades. The lawn was scarred with weed and, fortunately for Peter and Ellie, the old rusted car chassis in his backyard and the collapsing back fence were shielded from their view by a row of melaleucas.

In a rare moment of sentiment and disclosure, he once spoke of a wife, 'pale and lissom', his words, unafraid of Ellie's presence in recalling the moonlight licking her bedroom nakedness. He never related what happened to her, though Peter could sense a heaviness, a sadness whenever Frank spoke of her. There didn't seem to be any children. If there were, he didn't mention them. His only recreation was an occasional visit to the local pub.

He'd greet passers-by with a resonant g'day as they hastened away, wary of stopping. Peter and Ellie knew that his days were far too long, and his nights were longer still, so they tried their best to show an interest. But not too much.

'And how are you, Frank?' Peter asked out of duty.

'I'm still alive.'

'Is that all…still alive?'

'What else is there?'

Peter nodded. He was about to answer, but didn't. He wasn't in the mood for verbal sparring with Frank.

Ellie was standing at the front door, smiling.

Ellie

She could tell he was worried, and it wasn't like him. Perhaps there was something he knew and wasn't telling her. Had the GP said something? Worry was infectious between people who loved each other, so she was concerned.

In the early days of their marriage, they'd be surprised to learn that one of them was thinking the same thing as the other. It would often happen on a long car trip, when Peter might say, after twenty minutes' silence, 'I was thinking of what might have happened to Frank's wife,' and Ellie would be amazed because she had been thinking the same thing. The day she received the news of her father's death on her mobile, not only could Peter read her emotion, he knew the reason for it.

She discussed it with her friends and realised she and Peter weren't unique. That sort of telepathy, or whatever it was, wasn't uncommon. Still, she believed that for them it wasn't just the occasional connection of thought some people experienced. Most of the time, she knew what he was thinking and didn't have to ask. And most of the time, she knew what he was feeling.

Sometimes, she'd make a joke of it by answering a question that had never been asked, or smile seductively, say 'All right' and take him by the hand to lead him upstairs.

She felt his concern now, and wondered if it was just part of the anxiety that grows with the years, a symptom of a broader fear of imminent mortality.

Her old school friend Paula had changed in retirement from a self-confident teacher with a reputation for troubleshooting to an anxious and frightened woman who was so unsure of herself she was unable to drive her car or make difficult decisions. The loss of her husband might have explained some insecurity, but she did have a daughter living with her who could have helped. The years had exacted their own arbitrary toll.

Now I'm getting anxious, she thought, and smiled. Peter has never been anxious like that before, and it's not surprising that he might just be a little concerned now.

She remembered the time Claire broke her arm rock climbing. It was at a rock-climbing venue where children were given harnesses and climbed a carefully constructed vertical wall with imitation rocks placed for their feet.

'I'd rather you didn't go, Claire,' Ellie told her.

'But Mum, all the kids…'

'What do you think, Peter?' She didn't wait for the litany of Claire's reasons.

Peter asked all the necessary questions and, after satisfying himself that it should be safe, ruled in Claire's favour.

It was a freak accident. A new employee was responsible when Claire fell. She hadn't checked the harness. Ellie was worried and hurried with Peter to the venue, where paramedics were attending to Claire.

'Do you think she'll be all right?' she'd ask him on the way. 'What if there are things wrong with her that we can't see?'

Claire was all right apart from the broken arm, but when thinking about it later, what impressed Ellie was his calm, the common-sense way he reacted.

'Accidents happen. Of course she'll be all right, El,' he'd said. 'A lot of children break something before they're adult. There'll probably be worse to come.'

She recalled his receiving an award at work for his relationship with clients, and the presenter calling him sane and urbane. She liked that. Sane and urbane. It captured him perfectly. Of course he was sane, but for her the word had a broader meaning. It meant balanced, reasonable, not given to caprice or flights of emotion. But he was no Plato, believing that reason strangled emotion in every situation. He was an affectionate partner and a generous lover. And urbane meant mannered, cultured, knowing what was appropriate behaviour. Perhaps that was part of being sane.

She was different, not so much in letting emotion rule her head, but giving it equal importance. They'd laugh and tease each other, exaggerating the difference.

'You can't give in to emotion all the time. That's a recipe for disaster. You need to stand back and consider what to do. Otherwise, people will take advantage of you.'

'You need to develop your feeling side. People are emotional, passionate, caring. It's a more realistic and a more human way to behave.'

'Emotion is fine, but too much can make you impulsive. It leads to doing the wrong things.'

'And relying on reason leads to being a cold fish.'

They'd end such repartee by laughing, hugging and telling each other they were complementary and wouldn't want anything to change. Though once when she suggested they go upstairs, he stroked his chin and replied, 'Now let me think about it,' as if testing the suggestion with reason. It soon became ritual.

When asked about her growing up, Ellie would answer that it was probably the same for most children at that time. She would then pause as though she thought better, and speak of her mother who was always there to support her, and her father who would tell her that she could be anything she wished. She'd then feel an uneasy sense of betrayal for not professing her love, or giving them credit they deserved. This became even more apparent to her in later years when she became a parent herself.

Born in Sydney, she attended state schools and did well. She had a sister, Amity, younger by three years. She'd tell Peter that it had been ideal because as big sister she was cast in the role of protector and nurturer, able to answer some of Amity's growing-up questions. This was particularly valuable in their teenage years when they both became interested in boys. She'd tease Peter by saying it was necessary practice for looking after him.

The small family size gave greater opportunities for intimacy. Problems, as long as they were not too personal, were discussed at the dinner table. All four had an intuitive knowledge of acceptable limits, and there were few arguments. Her parents were not unusual for the times: caring but not demonstrative.

She excelled at sport, representing her high school in softball and netball. After leaving school, she gained state selection for long-distance running. A scholarship allowed her to train as a teacher, a vocation she believed was her calling, and contrary to the normal run of things, she was given a city appointment rather than being sent to the country like nearly all scholarship holders. She was popular with the other teachers and her students. During that time, she had several boyfriends, but nothing serious.

'Just imagine, Peter,' she told him, 'I might have married some farmer in the west of the state and be milking cows at five thirty every morning.'

'And be constantly pregnant,' Peter quipped.

She saw the car returning from the family room window, and hastened to the front veranda. As he opened the car door, she could see he was either distracted or deep in thought, even though he'd later say he wasn't thinking anything at all.

'Everything and nothing' was his usual answer to the question. She heard Frank call out but couldn't hear what they said.

She always wondered how two different people became one, how two different backgrounds could lead to similar sensibilities. She didn't realise how glad she was to see him. But of course he was always going to come back. What was she thinking?

'Welcome home, stranger,' she sallied as he joined her at the door.

'Stranger…is that what I am? I've only been gone for an hour.'

Peter

It was only a month ago that Peter went to the fiftieth reunion of his high school year at Meadowbank Boys' High. It was strange seeing his old schoolmates again, at least those that remained, but after each ten-year span of reunions, he felt more remote from it all this time, a commentator, a biologist, or was it an anthropologist, reporting on the span of life from childhood to old age, the ravages of time, and the transition from innocence to experience, rather than seeing himself as part of the same narrative.

He remembered those who were always intent on reporting their presumed success, and those like Hevers wanting to disprove malignant teacher prophesies. Hevers had been the butt of Spurling's once a week prediction in physics: 'You have as much chance of passing the Leaving, Hevers, as I have of floating to Hell on an iceberg.' It became so much a part of the lesson that as soon as Spurling started his warning, the class would all join in.

'It was different this time,' he told Ellie when he arrived home. 'Not nearly as many there as last time…and it's not hard to guess why.'

'How was it different?' Ellie asked even though she knew the answer.

'Well, after the surprise of the first hellos, with all of us trying to identify the older lookalikes, and those who'd abandoned their schoolboy personas to look even more different than last time, there was an uncomfortable lull, like an awkward silence at a dinner party. I mean, what do you say to someone after all that time…what's happened to you in the last decade, mate…or, what's news? Anything's going to sound lame. We've all grown too far apart. The old camaraderie's not there any more. It hasn't been for years.'

'You didn't enjoy it, then?' Ellie asked.

'Not really. It was nice to see some of my old friends, but It saddened me. I suppose it wasn't all bad. Some still laughed when we heard about Hevers flooring the science master with the orange, and Bracey getting caught impersonating Wattling. I couldn't. It's so tired now. It's wearing a bit thin…a bunch of ageing men trying to recapture their lost youth.'

'We're all a lot older.' Ellie realised this sounded trite but didn't know what else to say.

There were a few seconds of silence.

'It's like holding a mirror up to yourself. I kept asking myself if I look as old as these old school friends, and I suppose I do.'

'I'm sure you look a lot better than most. You've worked at keeping yourself fit.'

'All so different now.' Peter was feeling nostalgic, and that made him garrulous. 'I remember the numbered desks in four rows of twin seats, how we had to answer questions rather than ask them, raise our hands to speak, stand when another teacher entered the room, start everything with sir or miss, chant all the rules and never challenge anything…and then the cane. Open your mouth and that was it. Whack. And Barlow. Bloody sadist. Kids aren't caned any more.'

'Well, thank heavens for that.' Ellie had heard most of it before, the less enlightened days of teaching that had left their mark, but Peter had needed to speak. He'd never been so depressed about the reunions before. He was silent now. She could tell what he was thinking.

Were these really the best years of my life, he wondered. Meeting after all this time only exposes the abyss between us, between the then and now. Fifty years ago, you could have thrown a blanket over the sameness of our lives and dreams. Life has without warning levered us apart. Our old legends, heroes and mythologies are no longer shared. History and culture have colluded over the years to frustrate our schoolboy memories.

'Do you think there'll be another reunion?' Ellie's voice was almost a whisper, as though she could predict the answer, and the reason for it.

'They read out the list of truants,' Peter continued with his own train of thought, not answering Ellie's question. 'That's what they called them. Truants. Someone's idea of a joke. Some of them I didn't know. Had to draw on my fast disappearing mental map of classroom seats. Of course some were in other classes. Neville Duff, I've never mentioned him before, prostate cancer, died last year. Aspery, used to go around with Hevers. Dead, but some mystery surrounding how. Some suggestion of foul play. Nicholson and Stead both died before the last reunion. There was a suicide in one of the other classes. Oh, and Timewell, he was there but not there if you know what I mean, had to be led around by Farmer.'

They were just names for Ellie, but this reunion had made an impact on Peter like none of the others. And it wasn't hard to guess why.

'Sport and sex and politics have been relegated to second place,' Peter continued after a brief pause. 'And always trumped by mortality,' he resumed. 'That's what a lot of the conversation was about, that and sharing common medical problems. Prostate. Arthritis. Hip and knee replacements. Heart. Depressing! And you told me yesterday, El, of your friend Jenny…in the bowel and terminal…waiting for her first grandchild. Sorry, Ellie. I shouldn't be doing this. I'm getting maudlin. The last thing I want is to upset you.'

Peter had stopped speaking and Ellie was aware of his darkening mood. 'The coming of age is what, eighteen or twenty-one?' she said, keen to express interest for his sake without changing the subject, and at the same time to rescue him from the path he was heading down, lighten the mood. 'So where does that leave us? Perhaps for age we need a qualifying word. Rather than old, it should be mature, something to give it a ring of common sense…like a fruity wine.'

'Yes.' Peter had nothing more to say.

They sat in silence. He'd never been more aware of the passage of years, and he knew the referral from the GP and the meeting with Enright had a lot to do with it.

His mind had begun to trace the beginning of each day. When Ellie, an early riser, had already gone downstairs to the kitchen, he would open the curtains on a world that marked the time with season's march, feel the stubble on his chin, comb his fingers through his greying hair, and obey his body's need for the bathroom for the second time that morning.

He'd see his long-dead father's eyes in the bathroom mirror and wonder if he was growing more like himself or those who'd gone before. The unmistakable face of time would stare back.

Enough of this, he said to himself. It was the same for everyone. It was the simple and inevitable mark of age. There was no point wallowing in self-pity. It was as natural to the human condition as men having to shave or women being the ones to bear children. Old age had no favourites, and if you had a family like his, it did have its recompenses.

Ellie was sitting patiently, waiting.

'I'm sorry, El. I'm sorry you had to listen to my going on like that. I know I'm lucky,' he said. 'So very lucky.' And he put his arm around her shoulders. 'Others our age count the liver spots, devour their cache of pills, ride a bicycle or wear a broad-brimmed hat, and some probably feel a tenderness that loiters inside them, waiting to pounce. I don't do any of that, and what's more I have you, Ellie.'

'And I'll always be here for you, and there's nothing – what did you call it, lurking, or was it loitering? – inside and waiting to pounce. The scan will prove that. Come on, time for bed.'

As they undressed, climbed into bed and pulled the sheet over them, Peter made one further observation. For Ellie, it wasn't a non sequitur.

'You know, Frank has never thought of a reason for being here. Can't see beyond his own nose. I spoke to him once about the ancients' damning of the unexamined life, asked him about his view of life. You should have seen the look on his face. All Greek to me, he said, pleased with how witty he was.

Ellie didn't have to ask what prompted Peter's comment. She turned out the light and the silence was complete.

His early childhood years in the house at Epping were happy. His father and mother were doting parents, and his sister Susan, three years older, prided herself on being like a second mother.

Memory isn't always an act of will. It often creeps up, selecting sometimes indiscriminately from the covert store of history. Peter remembers the beach holidays at Forster, as regular as clockwork in the first week of January, and how his mother would run with him along the water's edge, laughing helplessly, her hair streaming behind, trying to kick his soccer ball and missing. He can still see her cheeks pinked by exertion and glistening, her eyes alight.

His father, much older than her, more grandfatherly, a benign gentleman of the old world, would sit on a folding chair reading, and smile at their pleasure.

And there was singing the forgotten favourites at the piano in his sweet soprano as Aunt Nancy laboured with the chords, 'It's a Sin to Tell a Lie', 'Daisy, Give Me Your Answer Do', the card games with the whole family sitting around the dinner table at his vanilla-scented Aunt Madge's house.

When later asked if his childhood was happy, he would answer yes, and although he'd talk of his schooldays with pleasure, and tell of the old school friends he still had fifty years later, his most enduring memories were of his sister Susan.

But there was a memory that was always invited in, one that was called on when the need to be selfless was important. It was the sound of his mother making the porridge at six a.m. in the kitchen beyond his bedroom door, a simple act that became a symbol of her dogged giving. There were many such memories but that one assumed a special status.

He was well-liked at primary school, playing the playground games that young children fashioned to their own ends, taking turns at controlling the action, but being careful to share. At high school, his very normality made him popular, bright without being brilliant, athletic and strong without being a world-beater.

'I think I was lucky,' he once told Ellie. 'I was able to straddle the different school peer groups, the different subcultures.'

His third high school year was significant in the history of his life. It was a maths class in the period before lunch, and Mr Burns stopped in the middle of an explanation at the chalkboard to join the principal who'd beckoned him from the doorway. Their faces were serious as they whispered to each other. The class was silent, curious, something was afoot. They stopped whispering and glanced his way.

'Peter,' the principal called softly. Not Allthorpe but Peter.

Several months later, his mother had remarried, a man who was two years younger who had recently divorced. He was caring but not loving, at least not in the way Peter understood, and the house was never the same. There were no heated challenges to authority that step-parents meet as children test the limits, but rather a coolness and, for Peter, an emptiness. His mother had also changed. He wasn't sure how, but there was less laughter. She seemed more burdened.

Susan left immediately she'd finished school, or some time before, and Peter's emptiness was more profound. His reaction to her leaving then, and to it continuing through the years, amazed Ellie.

'But you were so close. Surely she told you where she was going.'

'I suppose she was so anxious to get away, to leave it all behind. She might have thought I'd tell my mother, not that I would have. She might have planned to tell me later.'

'And she didn't?'

'No.'

'And what about your mother? She didn't know…didn't hear anything later?'

'No.'

'Peter, you don't think that's strange.'

'We were disappointed…let's be honest, we were hurt…wondered if she was upset with Mum marrying again so quickly. We thought that was the most likely explanation. But our real worry was whether she was all right. Anything could have happened to her.'

'Well, something mustn't have been right in her world. A girl of those tender years doesn't just get up and go without a good reason. You've always said she was like a second mother to you. If she was upset with her mother, why didn't she contact you.'

'Perhaps I was a part of that world she needed to get away from.'

'What's harder to understand, Peter, is that nothing seems to have happened in the last fifty years. Am I right in thinking that neither you nor your mother have done much to track her down? Don't you want to know if she's had a good life…or if she still has a life at all?'

'We tried early on. We found all the Allthorpes, but not her. And I don't know, Ellie, it might sound lame to you, but we figured she'd changed her name and didn't want to be found.'

'Don't you regret it now, Peter…after all these years?'

'Yes…over the years there were a few times…and I remember when Mum was dying a few years ago, and her mind was going, she'd keep asking "Where's Susan?" I'd tell her Susan was on her way. She knew I was there but…that really upset me. You never know when the end is coming…always think there'll be plenty of time…but when you know time is really running out…'

Questions like these – Peter saw them as interrogations – had taken place over the years. The most recent was a few months ago.

'I remember the last time we spoke about this you told me your mother kept asking about Susan. That made me really sad…poor woman, knowing her son was there when she was dying but not her daughter. Have you thought any more about…'

'Ellie, I know you're trying to help, but…look, if I thought Susan was in the least bit interested…'

'But what about you, Peter…aren't you interested? Your mother has been gone for a few years now. I don't want you to find yourself in the same position.'

'I suppose I'm a little scared, Ellie,of what she might be like if I ever found her. It might not be happy families, a happy reunion. It might be like the last few school reunions, or worse. We might have nothing in common. Better to feel pain than to feel nothing. I mightn't like what I see. It might be better to leave things alone.'

Ellie would retreat from these talks, but she couldn't help think that Peter was being evasive. Perhaps he was right, and it was better to preserve happy memories than resurrect a suspect reality.

Peter also left home after school, living in university accommodation as he studied law at Sydney University. He made a few close male friends and worked hard, but there were very few girl students in the Law Faculty at that time, and limited opportunities for anything but work. He did make regular weekend visits home where his mother lectured him for wasting away and not looking after himself.

Ellie joked with one of her girlfriends about his choice of vocation. 'If ever a job was tailor-made for someone…sanity,' and she winked.

'Urbanity,' her friend replied and laughed.

They'd had this talk before.

Ellie was his first real girlfriend.

Ellie

'Dogs.'

'I beg your pardon?'

'Dogs. I was at the North Sydney markets one Saturday in February and saw these two golden retrievers with their owner. They were magnificent. I went to pat them, and this man arrived a fraction of a second before me, and started to fondle them first.'

'And that was Peter.'

'That was Peter. We were admiring these dogs, patting them and talking to the owners.'

'And to each other.'

'Of course, Trish. He told me he loved dogs, and I could see he did. I do too, I said. Well, that's something we have in common, he said, and looked a little embarrassed.'

'Why? What's to be embarrassed about?'

'I could tell why. He thought he was being presumptuous, making it seem like we were similar, like we could share things, I suppose.'

'Like chatting you up.'

'Something like that.'

'How weird. What did you think…or feel?'

'I liked it. I really liked it. I found it endearing that he'd be so sensitive to what I might think.'

'So what did you do?'

'I rescued him, not that he needed it. Told him I was looking for a particular kind of lamp base, old-fashioned Victorian, and had he seen one. When he said no, I asked if he'd like to walk around the markets with me and look.'

'For a lamp base?'

'Oh Trish. I wasn't looking for a lamp base.'

'You scheming so-and-so, Ellie Allthorpe.'

'But it was so much fun. I can name you every stall we visited, handbags, boots, shrubs, towels, chocolates and endless stalls of cheap jewellery and tawdry dresses. And believe it or not, we found a stall selling lamps and bases.'

'Let me guess. The one you wanted wasn't there.'

'Right. I made a little show of being disappointed. I think he might have guessed by then. But the weather was great, hot and blue, you could hear birds singing and smell the scent of gardenias.'

'Ellie…already?'

'Yes, Trish. I knew then. No doubt about it.'

'And there was me having met hundreds, well, dozens of men and still hadn't found the right one. Lucky you. Go on.'

'It was afternoon and the stalls were packing up. We exchanged phone numbers, said we'd contact each other.'

'And you did?'

'I waited for three days and didn't hear. I'd jump every time the phone rang. So I decided to call myself.'

'Very forward of you, Ellie. Did you ever think he might have lost interest?'

'I convinced myself he hadn't. Don't ask me how I knew, but I reckoned behind that façade of manly assurance was an uncertain little boy, a little boy needing to be led. So I decided to ask him to dinner, using the excuse that the people next door had a border collie and a Labrador we could visit. Tried to make it sound casual, natural.'

'And he believed that, I mean that the dogs and not you were the attraction?'

'Not sure. I never asked.'

'Are you sure, Ellie, that behind your façade of confidence there wasn't an uncertain little girl?'

If the dinner was meant to be casual, there was nothing casual in her preparation. She planned the menu days before, and kept changing her mind about what to wear. Does that show too much leg? Does that make my bottom look big? Does red make me look washed-out? She settled on a classic knee-length black dress, and simple pearl earrings.

He arrived in caramel slacks and a sky-blue shirt, bringing a bottle of wine. 'I don't even know if you drink,' he began. 'With your love of sport, you might…'

'I do,' she interrupted, feeling a little tension. But was it his or hers?

'I didn't know if I should bring red or white. I wasn't sure what we might eat…' and he realised his presumption. If he'd asked, it would seem like he was checking on whether it suited his tastes.

'It's perfect.' She could see his dilemma. 'Come in. Come in,' she repeated, and ushered him into a large lounge area where a table was set with a white lace tablecloth, maroon napkins in ornate silver rings, and gleaming silver cutlery. Candelabra graced the centre of the table.

He looked surprised, perhaps a little uncomfortable with the formality, and for the first time she realised her preparation might be over the top, a little more than was necessary for a casual meal and a meeting with dogs.

'You look lovely,' he told her.

'So do you,' she answered quickly, and turned away in embarrassment. Men weren't lovely. Handsome perhaps.

'Different from the other day at the markets,' he continued with his praise, and it was his turn to be embarrassed. What was he implying… that she hadn't looked lovely before?

After a few seconds of awkward silence, Ellie clapped her hands in a teacherly way. 'Right,' she said, standing in front of him like she might have done with her third class. 'Let's start again. My name is Ellie Winton,' and she reached out her hand.

'And I'm Peter Allthorpe.' He followed suit, looking relieved and reached out to shake her hand.

They laughed and relaxed, both realising they were trying too hard, and the evening proceeded smoothly. He praised the dinner. She praised the wine, and they chatted about what they'd seen at the markets.

'The Kirribilli markets are on this Saturday,' he said. 'Perhaps we might find the lamp base you want.'

Was it just the hint of a smile she saw? Did he know the lamp base story was a hoax? Perhaps it was his forced casual way of wanting to see her again.

They left the table to sit on the lounge for coffee. 'So what about the dogs?' he asked.

'I'm sorry,' she queried, and realised she'd asked him here to see next door's dogs. She'd been so attentive in her preparations, she'd forgotten the feeble reason she'd given for asking him.

'Oh, I'm sorry,' she said again, 'next door have gone away and taken the dogs with them. I hope you're not too disappointed.' To say any more would have been protesting too much. She needed to change the subject of the dogs, and decided being direct was the best way forward. 'Peter, what did you think when I invited you to walk around the markets with me?'

'I was pleased. I thought you were really nice. And I enjoyed myself.'

Ellie was pleased. What more could she have expected him to say? 'And when I invited you to dinner?'

'Well, I thought the dogs…'

'Peter,' she said, placing her coffee cup on the table and leaning gently against him, 'next door hasn't gone away, I'd honestly forgotten about the dogs, and I promise that is the last lie I will ever tell you.'

Peter was touched. He'd always known the dogs were an excuse for the dinner invitation, and lie seemed too strong a word to use to cover her tracks for such a small *faux pas*. He was well aware of her manoeuvring to change the subject, and felt closer to her for being honest. Ellie realised that in her commitment not to fib again, she was letting him know she hoped for more. Good, she thought. So be it.

They didn't go to the Kirribilli markets, but he did invite her to Borrelli's, an Italian restaurant in Epping, the following Tuesday night. They were both dressed more casually as if the need to impress wasn't uppermost any more. They were comfortable with each other and laughed about the other night.

'How are the dogs today?' he asked with a poker face that changed to a grin.

She punched him gently on the shoulder.

'We were like the bashful hero and heroine in an 1890s music hall,' she laughed, 'all embarrassment and innocence.' But it had intrigued Ellie. She wasn't the timid sort. It was so unusual to behave the way she had. She knew what was happening, she told Trish, though she doubted if anyone could ever be prepared for it. Then, sitting across the table, she wondered if he felt the same.

She'd sworn she'd never lie, and she knew she never would, but that didn't mean you had to reveal your real feelings, particularly if you were never asked. She'd have liked to tell him what she felt, and she could do so now without embarrassment, but she didn't want him to feel uncomfortable. And such admissions nearly always called for a like response. She didn't want to put him in that position.

They walked back to her apartment arm in arm. The moon was brilliantly white and perfectly round like Giotto's circle. Stars smiled fondly on them from a cerulean sky. The night was still. She'd later recall it as one of those times when silence was to be prized, and talk was an assault on the natural world.

They halted at the gate and she kissed him, a kiss that carried a gentleness and sweetness rather than an urgency. They both knew this was a beginning, and not an end.

She'd later think of how some events, even tragic ones, could be a catalyst. Her father's sudden death was a surprise for the family. He hadn't been sick. He'd hardly ever been sick. Ellie's mother couldn't wake him one morning. There never was a satisfactory medical explanation.

The call came for Ellie when she was with Peter at Church Point. He saw her pale, and her lips tremble, knew something was wrong, guessed what it was, and hurried to hold her. She returned his hug with one arm while holding the phone in the other hand. They drove to her mother's in silence.

She needed him in the weeks that followed. And his need was as great as hers. He admitted to feeling the pain. They were inseparable throughout her incantations of bereavement and at the funeral where

Ellie insisted on paying tribute to her father, and spoke with great feeling and intelligence. She needed to be held. So did Peter.

It was years later they'd talk about that time and its significance. Ellie called him her rock, and shocked him by apologising for being self-centred. 'But think of what you've just been through,' he said, amazed. She'd already told him she'd always known he was the one.

Peter spoke of his need to be with her, and his frustration at not being able to shoulder the pain and bear it for her. He was surprised by his feelings and in awe of her quiet strength. She bore her suffering with dignity. She was no wilting violet, no helpless music hall heroine.

From that time, Peter was warmly welcomed by Amity and Ellie's mother, and he was spending most nights with Ellie. They'd sit on the lounge or lie on her bed. Tragedy proved a source of talk on the meaning of life, on love and faith and death, on shared vulnerabilities, talk that for most couples might have been thinly spread across many years, if at all.

Another event loomed large in the history of their romance. A month after the funeral, an old school friend of Ellie accused her of having stolen a bracelet at a school fundraiser they'd attended the night before. Peter saw Ellie's distress and, knowing she would never have done such a thing but might have taken it by mistake, was quick to confess that he might have done so, and that he'd search for it when he went back to his place.

'No, you couldn't have, Peter.' Ellie didn't say why. 'It must have been me when I was putting things back in my bag. You might remember, Joan, that I dropped it on the floor and some of my things fell out. I might have it at home.'

Neither would let the other take the blame.

Joan called the next day to apologise. 'I'm so terribly sorry. I feel awful.' She'd found the bracelet trapped in the lining of her bag.

Ellie was always intrigued by how an accident of circumstance, or a single decision could change a life. She'd always known that her future was bound up with Peter's, but was this the final blow to his carapace of restraint? It was for her.

Carolyn

A week after Peter's visit to Enright, it was Oliver's first day at school, and the family gathered in the front yard for photos. First, Oliver, pale, his neatly parted hair wetted to lie down, with the frightened look of the approaching unknown.

'Smile, darling,' Carolyn called. 'This is exciting. Oh God,' she whispered as pride and protectiveness struggled together, 'isn't he adorable?'

Perhaps it isn't exciting for him, Peter thought, but he smiled good-naturedly. Ellie was all smiles. These photos were important for posterity. He'd taken them for both the girls, Carolyn in her little tartan skirt, with one sock up and the other down, excited by the adventure he and Ellie had made it out to be, and Claire, neat, biting her lip, and apprehensive. Siblings were always so different.

'Now with your mother, darling. Daddy will want to see how happy you are. So one of your best smiles. Will you do the honours, Peter?' and she handed him the camera.

Carolyn lived a few suburbs away, and her husband Brian was overseas on business for a few weeks. She had decided to stay with the rest of the family while he was away. It was an opportunity to see more of her father. Claire was still single and lived with her parents.

'Now how can we all be in one?' She was gushing. 'Frank,' she called. 'That's his name, isn't it?' she whispered to Peter. 'Would you mind,' holding the camera towards him.

Frank had emerged from his front door and was watching, wondering what the fuss was about. 'What do I do?' he asked. 'How's this thing work? You'll have to show me.' It was obvious that he was secretly pleased to be included, part of the family.

That may have been a mistake, Peter and Ellie thought, but how was Carolyn to know? They were right.

'Thought I'd come and give the young 'un some advice on his first day,' he said, full of his importance.

Peter and Ellie looked at each other warily.

'Take it from someone who knows my boy,' he cautioned, grasping Oliver's shoulder so hard it made him wince. 'Don't let the other kids bully you. They'll try to! Make sure you stand up to them. Don't take a backward step. I never did.' With a self-satisfied look, he turned to Peter. 'Am I right, Pete?'

'Sure,' Peter said dismissively, giving him a cold look, and as Frank, the fount of all wisdom, having taken several photos of the sky and the family from their waists down, strolled away oblivious to his cool reception, Oliver began to cry. Carolyn, looking daggers at Frank's retreat, held Oliver as Ellie offered support, and searched for the sweet, the infant's cure-all she always carried in her pocket.

'It's going to be real fun, Oliver,' Carolyn comforted. 'You're going to make some real good friends. You can bring them home or to Pa and Granny's place if you like for special ice cream. Won't that be good?'

Carol would always remember the vivid image of Oliver's blue eyes, made both bluer by the crisply pressed blue school shirt, and wider with the uncertainty that would begin his life's academic journey.

The children and their parents were milling about the kindergarten rooms, the teachers showering them with dulcet words or sing-song asking names and patting heads that were sometimes turned tearfully to hide on mother's hip.

Carolyn spoke softly to Oliver, her eyes blinking with tears, embarrassed, and laughing at her silliness. 'They look like lovely rooms, Oliver. Look at all the mobiles hanging from the ceiling, and I can see lots of coloured pictures on the walls. And there's a nice grassy area over there with places to sit and lots of things to play on.'

Peter was strangely subdued.

For the past three weeks, there had been a number of induction days for the new arrivals. The children had met all four kindergarten teachers, and they had been taught a very simple lesson by each of them on a different day. It was often just the reading of a story with the children sitting on a mat at the front of the classroom, and the teacher including them by asking questions. 'Why do you think Mr Bear was happy?' 'What do you think might happen next?' Sometimes there were 'fun' activities and pictures to draw.

The mothers spoke to each other sharing what they knew about each of the teachers and wondering who might best suit their child. One was stern but fair, one was a lot of fun but did the important work get done? Another was a little alternative and did a lot of art. They'd only been told the day before what teacher their child would have. It must have been a lottery.

Oliver had already made a friend. His name was Nicholas, and his mother was friends with Carolyn. Oliver wanted them to be in the same class.

A bell sounded and the children and parents hushed. One of the teachers welcomed them, telling the children of the exciting times ahead, and they moved to their rooms. The children hadn't yet learned the way to line up, didn't know what it meant to line up. That would come later. Many looked apprehensive. Some didn't look back. A few did and waved.

Oliver disappeared through the first of many doors he'd meet over the years. He'd turned bravely to wave.

Quiet, and a thick nostalgia permeated the air. Parents stared, waited for a minute and retreated reflectively. Carolyn was dabbing at her eyes with a tissue. Peter and Ellie were left with brimming thoughts of old schooldays.

For Peter, it was a rite of passage, and while innocence like beauty shared the enemy of time, it was a necessary fate. He saw himself entering the door of a liver-coloured building a life ago wearing the identical sky blue shirt and grey shorts, a scab on his knee, feeling important because his new teacher, Miss Stenning, had chosen him to hold his hand, searching the sea of faces behind him for his mother. Some things never change. Others do.

Carolyn was anxious throughout the day, and even thought of standing outside the school fence at lunchtime to see if he was in the playground. She'd had no lunch herself and waited outside the school for twenty minutes before the final bell to collect him. Other mothers were also there.

'It went well, I hope. No tears, no scene?' Ellie asked when they returned home.

Carolyn was delighted and anxious to report. 'Oliver was excited when he met me at the school gate. He loves his teacher and he's in the same class as Nicholas. And I like Rosie, his mother. We can compare notes. We already plan to meet for coffee.'

'Look, Pa.' Oliver rushed into the room waving a sheet of paper. 'Look what I drew. Miss Briggs said to make a picture of our family to take home.'

Peter looked. 'Wow, Oliver, that's really good. That one looks just like me.'

'No, Pa, that's Granny, not you.'

'Brings back memories, doesn't it?' Peter said when Oliver had gone to share his drawing with Claire. 'Remember how we had to drag Claire kicking and screaming?'

'And before long she'd have been kicking and screaming if she couldn't go to school. You keep feeling you want to help, but what more can you do? They're so innocent, so vulnerable.'

'Just like you were as a grown man, Mr Allthorpe. Romance's bumbling hero aflutter near his heroine. A shy romantic with his actions stilled by fear. Do you know how hard it was to get you to notice me, I mean really notice me?'

'But look at me now, Mrs Allthorpe. No vulnerability now, and as for innocence…'

'Don't look at me like that, Mr Allthorpe.'

'I think sometimes of how you had to make the nativity scene at school.' Peter was suddenly serious and emotional now. 'You were only six, and your mother wasn't well and couldn't help, so you made it yourself from a torn shoebox and paper cut-outs you coloured in of a shepherd and grazing sheep, grubby cotton wool for snow. And the nun who did the judging, she walked around all the exhibits, some grand, obviously made by parents, painted and wrapped in cellophane and glitter with carved animals for the manger. That nun, you don't even remember her name, who stopped at your shoebox and said that Joseph and Mary didn't have a thing. This one says it all, she said. She chose yours. I'm still moved when I think of that.'

'But why?'

'I'm not sure. The nun who looked beyond the obvious to see what's really important, and your own innocence not just then, a sort of enduring innocence, a welcome lack of worldliness.'

'Me innocent…unworldly?' Ellie was surprised. 'Are you serious?'

'Yes, of course I am. I'm probably using the wrong word, but I mean innocence as being blameless, doing right, being virtuous.'

'Well, I'd better see to the dinner,' she said softly, visibly moved. At the door, she turned. 'I love you, you know.'

'Really?' he queried with mock surprise.

She poked out her tongue and darted away smiling.

After Carolyn had read to Oliver and settled him down for the night, she went looking for Peter and found him in the comfy chair on the veranda looking towards the far hills, a blur of charcoal, a book open and face down on his lap with his reading glasses. He stood as she joined him.

'I was hoping you'd be here,' she said, and embraced him.

They held each other for a long time, her head resting against his shoulder. There was no need to say anything.

Peter

'Hello, Dana.' The carroty-haired receptionist's name was on a name tag fixed to her neatly pressed blouse below the collar. He hadn't noticed it on his first visit.

'Morning, Mr Allthorpe. What a lovely day. Dr Enright won't be long.'

She watched as he sat down, and his fertile imagination wondered if there was some meaning in her being so pleasant, the fanciful bent of the mind to find ironies. Perhaps she only wanted to see if he'd do his fish imitations again.

He was the only patient in the waiting room, and the MRI had been done several days ago, all cold efficiency, sliding into a tubular chamber with lights and lots of whirring and metallic noises. He felt he'd been the numbered subject of a space-age experiment. The results had already been sent to Enright. There'd also been an additional blood test.

He was worried, but had told Ellie that the tests were regulation, that Enright was known to be particularly thorough, more so than was necessary, and that there was no need for her to come. He had waived away her protests.

She had hugged him and walked with him to the garage. 'I'll be here when you get back,' she'd said. 'Now don't get into any mischief.'

'I'll do my best,' he answered.

Carolyn and Claire had joined them, but didn't want to make an unnecessary fuss and make him anxious. They had no reason to think it was a big deal, so they wished him good luck with a farewell kiss.

Oliver, oblivious to such things, and with the infant's unshakable belief in permanence, had said there'd be another picture of him when he returned home from school, and this time there'd be no doubt it was him because his hair wouldn't be green. He'd left an hour ago.

The drive was pleasant. The day was warm like most others at this time of the year. Frank was asleep in his veranda chair, his chin resting on his chest, his mouth wide open. A good sign. No accounting for his movements necessary.

He passed Lorna Atkins walking her two black Labradors. He waved. Seeing the prancing dogs always brought a smile to his face. Two girls with long ponytails were playing hopscotch in their driveway. Autumn had arrived and the liquid ambers were already turning russet. Gold coin from poplars zigzagged to the ground. The natural world gave no clues about what lay ahead.

He entered Enright's rooms unaware of having driven at all, not even remembering the walk from the parking lot. It felt as if he'd been picked up and put down there.

He'd only just sat down, wondering what had happened to the rheumy-eyed woman with the scans on her lap, when Enright opened his door.

'Come in, Peter,' he said quietly, and moved aside to allow Peter's entry.

'Peter,' he'd said, and with the use of his first name, Peter was instantly on guard. They'd only met once before. Weren't doctors usually more formal? Was it a statement of sorts? Enright motioned to the patient's chair, and this time he sat behind his desk.

The room was just as he remembered it, the high bench or bed covered in sheets of paper towelling, the row of cupboards along one wall, and a gleaming washbasin in one corner. The instruments of a surgeon's trade were not apparent, and the clinical atmosphere was warmed by the autumn shadings of the furniture and blinds. A photo of a dark-haired woman with an arm around each of two smiling children was conspicuous on his desk.

'It's not the best of news, I'm afraid.' Enright knew from his years of experience that in moments like these it was better not to start with pleasantries, but get straight to the point. 'It's non-Hodgkin lymphoma. High-grade,' he added, not averting his eyes.

Three seconds of reporting that for Peter changed the course of the world.

Enright, sensitive to the impact of his news, hurried to explain. 'It's a cancer that attacks the white blood cells called lymphocytes, part of the body's immune system.'

Peter heard the voice droning years away as Enright explained, a blowfly circling on the overhead light. He floated beyond himself as if he wasn't the sole agenda after all. When the voice stopped, he wasn't sure what to ask, the palpable stillness as heavy as a summer eiderdown that needed to be tossed aside.

'How long?' he asked.

The answer was predictably evasive. It was impossible to be definite.

'It's important that I know, doctor,' Peter said, 'because…' He didn't continue.

'It is high-grade, very aggressive, which surprised me,' Enright was quick to answer, 'because apart from some minor swelling in the lymph nodes under the armpits, and your tiredness, there are usually more obvious symptoms. But in answer to your question, there is a reasonable survival rate. It is high-grade, and that's not good, but new treatments are introduced all the time, new medicines.' He stopped short of saying miracles happen.

'I understand.' Peter was trying to be patient. 'But survival rates aside, what would be a typical time,' and then more quietly, 'time I might have left?'

'About twelve months, possibly fifteen,' Enright answered, this time with no evasion. Perhaps twelve months was meant to sound better than one year. Strength in actual numbers.

'So what happens now?' Peter felt helpless, like a child waiting to be led.

'I'm not sure that stem cell replacement is the way forward. It will certainly mean chemotherapy, possibly radiation, and the sooner the better. I can make an appointment today. There are several oncologists here at the hospital.'

Peter remembered needing Ellie as he'd never needed her before. She'd have asked the questions he later regretted not having asked, like how would the cancer progress, were there exercises or a special diet, would he be helpless for much of that time, and what would the end be like?

She would have made it clear then and there that it was something that had happened to both of them, and that they'd deal with it together.

He left Enright's rooms, not hearing Dana's cheery 'Goodbye, Mr Allthorpe' or seeing her look of concern when he didn't answer.

He wandered down the soft linoleum corridors of the hospital and took a lift till he found himself in the hospital cafeteria. He was anxious to get home but he had taken a wrong turn and thought that a coffee might settle him.

He was thinking of Oliver's face superimposed on his own as he entered his kindergarten room a life ago, fresh and unvintaged. His thoughts flowed to his recent school reunion, imagining his own name being read out with the list of truants to a hushed audience. 'Yes, Allthorpe,' someone would probably say, 'nice fellow, a prefect, sat next to Watson.'

Gulping down his lukewarm and bitter coffee, he emerged into the bright sunlight of mid-morning. His shock was now mantled by a reactive show of common sense. His defences were already springing into action. I'll do this well, he thought. I'll make my death a crowning glory of my life.

Driving home, his thoughts and feelings jumped about like marbles in a shaken tin can as he contemplated how to reorder a life and make new priorities. The first step would be to make sure that Ellie and the girls were comfortable for the rest of their lives. And then of course there was Oliver's schooling to think of. There'd probably be no cricket with him in the backyard now.

And then there were his own plans. What did people call them? A bucket list. The plans he'd harboured for years that would never be realised. The book he wanted to write on the history of the local area, the class on art appreciation he'd planned to attend with Ellie, auditioning for a major part in the local amateur theatre's performance of a Noel Coward play.

He was home remembering nothing of the drive. Thankfully, Frank wasn't on his veranda. He couldn't face that. Ellie was standing on the front steps, waiting for him. Her look of pleasure flickered, died.

Ellie

Ellie had been led to believe that Peter's second visit to Dr Enright was routine. She had wanted to go with him but he seemed intent on going alone. She was arranging flowers she'd grown for the family room when she had the strange sense he was nearby. It wasn't unusual for either of them to have that sense about each other. I prefer the yellow roses to the red, she thought airily. I wonder what Peter will think?

She went to the front door as the car turned into the driveway. But as it stopped in front of the garage door and she saw the way he got out, as if he were carrying the burdens of the world on his shoulders, she knew that all wasn't well.

Resisting the urge to confront him on the steps, she quickly led him inside without saying a word, sat him down, took his hand and waited.

'Not good news, El,' he began, and gave a faltering account of Enright's news. He told her everything including Enright's proposed treatment and his estimate of the time he more than likely had left. Ellie was stunned. Her face flamed as if it had been slapped, and she battled to find the consoling words, never taking her eyes from his.

'It's not all bad,' he continued, seeing her distress, and hurting as much from her pain as his own. 'Enright was hopeful. Said great advances are being made all the time. And the chemo, well, it might…' He realised how hollow his repeating of Enright's spiel sounded, the medico's necessary false comfort, the vestige of hope.

Shock, which briefly left her frozen, would send the wrong message to Peter, so she struggled to be upbeat, holding him, reminding him that they had always been a team and that they would face this hiccough together.

'A bit more than a hiccup, Ellie,' Peter replied with false cheer.

Drama could only increase the pain he read in Ellie's eyes. 'But I know you'll be there every step of the way.'

In the days and weeks that followed, Ellie was magnificent, refusing to entertain the negatives and give up hope. Even knowing that she was making a show of optimism for his sake, Peter was grateful, and the heaviness of his load was lightened. Sometimes, she was over-attentive, indulging him so much she unwittingly robbed him of the opportunity to help around the house and remain active, to feel he was contributing something.

She was well aware of the dangers of overindulging him, and magnifying the very impact of the prognosis she was intent on challenging. She knew that Peter feared being an invalid, and even more so being treated like one. So hers was a balancing act.

There was also the problem of making too light of the situation to save Peter from depression, and to conceal her own terror, the terror of losing him. She had to struggle against becoming depressed herself.

In those first months, her mind kept replaying his proposal all those years ago, the well-chosen words he later admitted were rehearsed, the sun on their backs as they waded in the warm green shallows at Church Point, his taking her hand and gently turning her so she wasn't squinting in the sun when he put the question. She'd had a few casual boyfriends, boys she went out with and nothing more. Some of them wanted more, and she'd had to weather the petty jealousies and recriminations.

It was all so different with Peter, the voltage of their mutual certainty, the current of their love.

It might be different now, she thought, but stronger and tougher than ever. Over the years, there'd been the odd fleeting disagreement, an occasional brief retreat, but their talking together about setbacks united them more strongly than ever. Her imaginings of what they shared weren't fanciful. This was no case of love's retrospective tendency of making a fiction of itself.

The girls were stunned when they arrived home after work to hear the news. Peter asked Ellie to let him tell them. He wanted to contain the spill of emotion for his own sake and theirs, wanted the message to be one of hope.

Carolyn cried, refusing to believe Enright's prediction. 'But you're so well,' she kept saying. 'You're fitter than men forty years younger.'

Claire was numb, already thinking of how she could help. Oliver wondered why no one was talking or laughing at the dinner table that night.

Ellie knew there would be no opposition from Peter about going with him to the oncologist. No secrets now, no going it alone, no machismo. She teased him that he hadn't spoken about his concerns after the first visit. 'It's so typically male,' she said. 'From now on, I'll be there with you for every appointment. No arguments!'

Carolyn and Claire were not there to see them leave in the morning of the first visit to the oncologist. They had wanted to be there for him, but Peter didn't want a fuss. It was serious, he didn't deny that, but he didn't want it blown out of all proportion by emotional farewells.

Dr Chang was a lean, antiseptic and softly spoken man with thinning black hair through which a fawn scalp shone. His rooms were sparsely furnished and clinical. The waiting room was off-white with functional black chairs lining two walls. There was no fish tank but there was help yourself coffee and tea, and a two-thousand-piece jigsaw puzzle half-finished on a table. All patients could contribute. Perhaps the painstaking effort needed calmed nerves, or served to promote the need for patience.

In the weeks and months that followed, if Ellie found Peter sombre, she would divert him with joking references to the blossoming romances reported in the waiting room magazines. The receptionist was at first unsmiling and business-like, and Peter found himself missing the smiling Dana and her carroty red hair.

They both answered 'Yes' in one voice when Chang asked if Peter would like his wife to be present. Ellie saw it as the start of a process of hope. Peter thought of it as a downward spiral, the beginning of a process with an inevitable, if delayed, conclusion.

Chang quietly explained the treatment. He would start by using CHOP, an acronym for a combination of four drugs. Others would be introduced as the treatment continued. Each cycle would last for several weeks, and the drugs could be administered at the hospital under Chang's supervision. The treatment would begin next week. 'Is there anything you'd like to ask?'

Peter was well prepared and asked several questions that Chang answered directly. Ellie was with him and was taking some notes. He no longer felt helpless as he had with that last visit to Enright. A time was set for the first treatment, and Chang gave them a thick folio of information.

Ellie had brought a thermos of coffee and home-made biscuits. Peter loved brownies. She wasn't prepared to face the hospital cafeteria. Neither was Peter. That might come after his treatments.

They drove to West Head, a majestic national park lookout high on a cliff with views of the waters of Broken Bay and the ocean, and sat on a wooden bench looking across the water to Palm Beach. A few yachts seemed to be barely moving below. A picture postcard. All was silent.

The sun blazed from a cloudless royal blue sky, threading the waters below with silver yarn. Gums with their canopies of shade sighed with a breath of eucalyptus when the wind blew in gentle breaths from the ocean. Several large lizards were basking on the sandstone rocks, prehistoric.

They didn't speak. They didn't have to ask each other what they were feeling. It was so very much bigger than them both.

Peter

In the weeks that followed, and throughout the first cycle of chemotherapy, Ellie was magnificent. She never uttered a negative word, and even though her high spirits were for Peter's benefit, she clung to hope, and faith. She cried, but was careful to do so when alone.

Throughout those weeks, there were many nights when Peter couldn't sleep, his thoughts painted black, when demons nested in his overactive mind, and holograms of the already departed, parents, relatives and friends, appeared like ghost train visions, one melting into another in an endless procession.

There were nights when he thought Ellie was asleep, and he'd escape barefoot to the front veranda, grateful for the coolness of the quarry tiles on bare feet, and suck in great gulps of air, a hunger for a life that couldn't be stored for rainy days.

He'd search the trees soughing gently in the sentient black beyond the house, inviting the fantasy that someone might be there with trumping rights to overturn his fate and listen to his silent plea.

These nights would often end with the sudden feeling of Ellie's arm around his shoulders, and her head resting in the hollow of his neck before they climbed the stairs wordlessly together arm in arm to tempt sleep again.

It took some time for the weight to ease for the family. Sometimes cheery hellos were too forced. Sometimes there was an uneasy silence. Ellie was the constant, always buoyant. Claire, ever practical, insisted on assuming some of Peter's work around the house. Often silent, nursing her hurt, she became skilled at using the petrol mower, but only when Peter was at his therapy and couldn't stop her.

Carolyn found it difficult to prevent her feelings from spilling over.

Family was her world, the only one she'd really known. Her father had always been there for her. She could still recall the times as a little girl that she'd had the flu, and her father would sit at the foot of the bed at night and read to her until she fell asleep. Sometimes, she'd wake for a moment as he pulled the blankets up under her chin and kissed her forehead. And there were all those times he sat in the old community hall watching her in the physical culture competitions.

During the first cycle of chemotherapy, she entered the study one night in tears. Peter was sitting at his desk, and stood as she came in. He was delighted to see her. She started speaking before he had time to welcome her.

'Carolyn, it's…'

'I've never told you enough, Dad…not nearly enough, I should have told you more just what…' And seeing the blush, the bitter-sweet of pleasure and pain spread across his face, his arms opening to receive her, she hurried from the room to her mother. 'I think I might have caused him more pain,' she cried.

'He'll understand, Carolyn,' Ellie replied. 'It will prove to be a real comfort for him as time goes by.'

It was never Peter's way to seek sympathy, or wallow in misfortune. Thanking the family for their concern and help, he gently suggested that he didn't want to be treated as an invalid, and began a book and internet search of the characteristics of his cancer and its likely progress. Chang had already given him a lot of information, but he wanted details.

His hair had already started to thin, even after the first round of chemotherapy, but apart from the immediate reaction to the therapy, he felt good. There was no nausea or diarrhoea, the quoted side-effects, and, as far as he could tell, no loss of strength or fitness. He was eating well and running three times a week, careful to avoid infections. He did get tired but that was easily explained.

He needed to set things right for the family, make sure they would all be provided for. The first step was Eugene Fowler, an old school contemporary, a lifelong friend and his financial adviser. He was distressed by Peter's news.

'Makes you wonder, doesn't it? I mean, look at me,' and he shifted his ample buttocks on the leather chair that was barely big enough to support him, 'and look at you, still running half-marathons. No rhyme or reason.'

Peter shrugged, avoiding the usual clichés about the arbitrary nature of life and lack of poetic justice. It wouldn't have been appropriate.

'Don't worry, Pete. Be assured, I'll look after everything here. Ellie and the girls will want for nothing.' And he levered himself from his desk chair and heaved his bulk around to face Peter, who had stood to leave.

There was an awkward moment as Eugene, his hands limp by his sides, wondered whether to hug his old friend. Might that be too melodramatic? Peter was thinking the same. They settled for a double-handed handshake.

His next visit was to his solicitor, a slight balding man who was more comfortable with documents than people, and who worked in the same legal firm Peter had belonged to years before. They shared the name of Peter. The old will was straightforward. Everything was left to the immediate family. Very few changes had to be made except some provision for Oliver's education.

A quiet period followed. All the important business was done, but for Peter that was a two-edged sword. It was good not to have things hanging over his head, but action was an antidote for idle and unwelcome thoughts.

'I have everything sorted,' he told Ellie. 'The will, the finances with Eugene, Oliver's education…even the repairs to the bathroom to be completed.'

Ellie listened. She knew there was more he had to say.

'But I'm not sure if I have that…what…that sense of quiet completeness…that sense of total peace that comes when…'

'Surely you have, darling. Don't you think we're all looking for more, never accepting where we are, never satisfied with what we have.

And that's not always a bad thing. Whenever we achieve something, we usually find there's another mountain to climb. But I can't think of anyone who has more reason to be at peace with the world.'

'You really think so?'

'You've always treated people kindly. You've done so much for so many. There's no need to apologise to anyone, no balance to redress.'

'I think you paint too glowing a picture of me.'

'All right, tell me who you have to make peace with.'

'Well, there was Terry Addison. When we were in fourth class, I pinched some of his marbles because he'd been mean. And I know I hurt little Jenny Dibley when I wouldn't go to the school formal with her.'

'Terrible! You wicked man, Peter Allthorpe! That will really damn you.' Ellie immediately realised her attempt to match Peter's typical joking was the wrong thing to say. She took his hand as tacit apology and hurried on. 'There's something else, isn't there, Peter?' she hastened to say. 'That's why we're talking, isn't it?'

'Susan.'

'Susan. Yes of course.'

'Big sister. I used to worship her, Ellie. When I did something I shouldn't have, she'd defend me. I remember breaking a vase, an expensive one, claret and gold, hand-painted from that glass-blowing place in Venice.'

'Murano.'

'Yes, Murano. When it came time to face my father, Susan took the blame. Said she'd knocked it off the table with her school bag.'

Ellie wouldn't interrupt. This had been a long time coming.

'When I was in first year high school, I had a mad crush on a classmate called Amber Wright. Funny, I remember the long straight hair, freckles, and braces on her teeth. I was smitten, and I suppose I was pathetic, mooning around feeling sorry for myself because she probably didn't feel the same. Susan could have teased me. She didn't. She helped me through all that. She must have been going on fifteen at the time, and helped me understand girls, told me what to do, never teased me.'

'I know I've asked before, Peter, but you have no idea why she left home? I know you said things weren't the same after your father died, but to disappear like that?'

'I don't know. Really. I've wondered if there was a boy, someone we didn't know about that she went to be with.'

'And now you think it's time to find out?'

'It's not so much that, El. There might have been no real reason. She might have needed a change of scenery, might have wanted a less insular life. She's the only other member of the family I have, and the only one I can't account for.'

'And finding out…that's part of, what did you call it, a quiet completeness? Like finishing the picture, completing the circle.'

'Yes, exactly that. We hear all the time about people dying who never had the chance to set things right, people who are killed or die suddenly, perhaps with things that have never been resolved, things they planned to get around to doing one day…and the thousands of people who die all alone in nursing homes or hospitals with no chance to say goodbye to someone who cares. That won't happen to me. I've been given a chance.'

'The chance to set things right,' Ellie said quietly, as much to herself as to Peter. 'A quiet completeness… I like that.'

'I do know, El, what I'm letting myself in for. It might be that she doesn't want to see me. It might be that she's dead. I know I might be disappointed at what I find, but I have to try.'

'You know I'll help in any way I can.'

'You're not annoyed then?'

'Annoyed? Peter, why would I be annoyed? I couldn't be more pleased. For years I've wondered.'

Ellie put her arm around his shoulder and pulled him to her. 'Just make sure she doesn't start to mother you again. That's my job.'

'Funny, Ellie, but I never really thought of you as my mother,' and he winked.

Carolyn

When they arrived at the holiday home in Ocean View Drive, Mrs Blythe was in the front garden pruning shrubs. More by design than accident. Living next door, she was paid by the owners to clean the house and do odd jobs when tenants vacated, and had been waiting for them. She was a jolly, heavily rounded woman with blonde curly hair and shiny pink cheeks. Peter thought she matched his image of an English barmaid.

Carolyn had organised a week away for the family a few days after the second round of Peter's chemotherapy. It was a break they all needed. The possibility of it being their final family holiday together was not lost on any of them.

It was the holiday house they rented each year, usually in January. It was an older brick home with dated furniture, a feature that attracted Ellie and Peter because the risk of their causing any damage wasn't as great. 'Lived-in,' Ellie described it. There was a short walk of a hundred metres to the beach, and a few hundred metres to the town.

It was six weeks after Peter's first visit to Chang, and Carolyn had returned to her own home, though she still spent much of the day with Peter and Ellie. Her husband Brian had also returned home, and was to join them on Friday evening and spend the weekend there before driving to work in the city on Monday morning.

Terrigal is a holiday haven on the central coast of New South Wales that is rapidly becoming the living choice for young couples and retirees. As a result, high-rise blocks of units are springing up, a happening that long-term residents and returning holidaymakers deplore, believing it is robbing the place of its unspoiled seaside charm.

A row of statuesque and towering fir trees line the esplanade and overlook the beach. Peter remembers seeing black and white photos of them in olive-coloured mounts, circa 1922, that he bought at a store of bric-a-brac at one of the town's market days.

A rectangle of streets, the town centre, runs parallel to the ocean, and is replete with coffee shops and boutiques, making it a mecca for weekend tourists. Several other townships, Avoca, Copacabana, Macmaster's Beach, Kilcare and The Entrance, each with their own beach, are only a few minutes drive away.

They arrived in two cars, Peter, Ellie and Claire in one, and Carolyn, Brian and Oliver in the other. Oliver darted from the car and ran to hug Mrs Blythe. She was a favourite, the valued dispenser of fantails and musk sticks.

'My, my, look how much you've grown, Oliver. What a big boy you are now. You're quite a little man.' She reached into a pocket and produced a packet of assorted sweets. 'Promise you won't eat them all now, Oliver, or your mother might get cross with me, and we wouldn't want that, would we?'

The adults were getting bags out of the cars. Brian and Carolyn were heading laden for the front door. They knew Mrs Blythe could be trusted with Oliver. She was almost part of the family.

'It must have been over a year since you two were here. You usually come in summer. Ellie, you haven't changed a bit. Age has been kind to you. But Peter dear, not so kind to you.' She laughed. 'You're going bald.'

'It's the worry, Connie, all the months of missing you.'

'Oh,' she chuckled.

They visited Kilcare on the first day and sat on the lawn outside the café that overlooks the beach in a wan sun with coffee and muffins for morning tea. A milkshake for Oliver.

'Autumn days can be hot in the sun and cold out of it,' Claire observed.

'Who wants to go for a walk along the beach?' Peter asked.

Ellie and the girls looked at each other and shook their heads.

'We're enjoying sitting in the sun, what there is of it.' Carolyn spoke for them.

'I'll come,' Brian answered.

'So will I,' said Oliver. He couldn't understand why sitting in the sun could have such appeal for grown-ups, and started to run down to the beach.

Brian was a well-built man. Carolyn called him muscular. He was in his late thirties with a full head of prematurely grey hair. Iron-grey rather than bleached grey, and that gave him a distinguished look. Peter and Ellie had always thought him to be guarded, as though he found it hard to let down his defences, answer the risky call of emotion. They'd heard that he was a tyrant in business, but he doted on Carolyn and Oliver and that was what mattered to them.

He walked with Peter along the water's edge, along the sand made hard by the water's flow and ebb, while Oliver darted ahead looking for shells and coloured stones. It was warm, and the sky was a pastel blue with anaemic threads of cloud. The ocean was a mass of glitter. Seagulls swooped and rose squawking in flight.

'I wanted to find time to talk,' Brian began, 'about you…and Carolyn. I guess you know she's really cut-up about your diagnosis.'

'I know,' Peter answered cautiously. He'd never had a real heart-to-heart with Brian before. 'I don't want her to suffer, Brian, no more than, well, no more than is normal…or appropriate.' He winced. 'Sorry, I hope that didn't sound selfish.'

'No, no, I know what you mean. I'd feel the same.' Brian felt the need to tread carefully. It was necessary he make this connection. And difficult. 'It's important she grieve. If she didn't suffer at all, it might call your relationship with her into question.' He paused. Had he said too much? 'You know, Peter, she thinks the world of you. And I know that when…well, when…'

They'd stopped as Oliver had found several coloured stones. A wave had washed over Peter's trainers. He watched as Oliver charged towards them.

'Dad, Pa, look at these. Look at the red one. Its shiny and it glows. Do you think it's worth a million dollars? I'll take them home and put them on my table.'

He was gone before Brian could answer, leaving him with a gritty handful of stones as he went searching for more.

'The first time we went out together,' Brian was grateful for the interruption, 'you might remember me coming to your house with those flowers, the ones that had their petals blown away in the wind on the way over…so embarrassing to give her what must have looked like a handful of stems… I asked her what sort of men she liked. I was fishing, I suppose, what sort of man she might end up with…and quick as a flash, she said someone like my father.'

'Is that right?' Peter was moved. Brian had never been so open about his feelings. He wasn't one for concessions.

'I suppose I understand Carolyn as well as anybody, perhaps with the exception of you.'

They were ambling together, their faces turned to the ocean, squinting in the sun that silvered the water.

'I wanted you to know, Peter, that I understand why she feels that way.' They'd stopped, and Brian turned away so Peter couldn't see his eyes.

'Of course I'm my own man, whatever the hell that means,' Brian continued, feeling the need to soften what sounded like a boast, 'but I've learned things over the years from observing you.'

'I don't know what to say, Brian. Thank you.' He resisted the temptation to ask what. 'I'm glad you're a part of our family, and I know Carolyn and Oliver will be well looked after.'

Brian nodded and they continued on their way. He'd said all that he needed to say.

Peter was in high spirits that night.

The days fell into a routine. Brian had returned to Sydney. Beach in the morning, a different one for the first four days, and home after a late lunch. Sometimes a walk in the afternoon, with Mrs Blythe looking after Oliver, who couldn't see the point in walking unless it led somewhere exciting. Twice they went out for dinner to a café on the Esplanade, and walked along the beach listening to the sounds of the ocean. On the other nights, it was pasta or takeaway pizza at home.

In the late afternoons, Peter would often go for a walk with Oliver along the beachfront. He looked forward to these times, as they were opportunities for him to share one-on-one with his grandson. They were times he could pass on…what, he wondered…what wisdom do you reveal to a child, and how? He settled on time alone. That was sufficient.

Each time they went, he'd buy Oliver an ice cream or chocolate bar, making him promise not to tell his mother. 'You have to eat your dinner, Oliver, or we'll both be in trouble.'

They both enjoyed the conspiracy.

'That man's caught a fish. Can we look, Pa?'

Peter and Oliver were walking along the boardwalk together towards the Skillion one afternoon. A fisherman had reeled in a large fish that floundered at the end of his line.

Oliver scampered away to watch, and returned a minute later looking troubled. 'Do fish die when they get out of water, Pa?' Oliver was frowning.

The man was removing the hook from the fish's mouth.

'Yes, they do, Oliver. They live in water like we live on land.' Peter could see him thinking, that same look of innocence he'd seen on his first day at school.

'Does it hurt them to die?' He was watching the fish being thrown into a hessian bag.

It's just as well, Peter thought, that the man wasn't slicing it open and cleaning it.

'It might hurt them a little.' Peter wasn't going to lie. 'But not too much.'

'Does it hurt us when we die, Pa?'

'Sometimes it does, Oliver. Sometimes it doesn't.' Peter knew that the answer would probably not satisfy Oliver, but how could he hope to explain that lives and deaths were very different? How could he explain that the world didn't operate on a system of poetic justice, that good people didn't always have good deaths, and bad people often didn't have bad ones? He could anticipate the question that would follow, the perennial why, and then even he might be out of his depth.

'Death is a part of life,' he said lamely, not sure why he said it.

'I don't want it to be part of mine,' Oliver replied.

The next day was cold. The sky was a leached milky blue as they walked to the beach at Wamberal. Clouds billowed, and they could feel the cold air blowing from the water, blowing the colour from the sky. The leaves from the liquid ambers carpeted the ground in a fibrous carpet of browning reds and golds, a sure sign of a dying autumn.

'Perhaps this wasn't such a good idea,' Claire said, pulling the hood of her jacket over her head.

'We needn't stay,' Carolyn suggested, 'but we've come this far, and it'll be worth looking at the ocean. I reckon the waves will be big.'

The sand was damp and unyielding as they entered the path to the beach, and sat in the lee of a mass of acacia shrubs. But they offered no protection from the wind swirling from the waves and blowing a gauze of sand.

'Perhaps we should turn back, get a coffee at the café,' Ellie suggested.

'Who's for a swim?' Peter called, standing and tugging at his belt buckle.

'You have to be kidding.' Carolyn thought he was joking. He wasn't.

'Peter. Don't be silly. It's nearly winter. Of all the days to go swimming.' Ellie was careful in the words she chose. Peter had been more sensitive lately, more likely to suffer hurt by what he saw as a challenge. Silly wasn't as harsh as mad.

But Peter had stripped to his costume. He had obviously decided to swim before they left home.

'In your condition, Dad, you shouldn't…' Claire began, and realised her remark was a tactic Peter wouldn't appreciate. The reminder he wouldn't appreciate. Red rag to a bull.

'Please don't, Dad,' Carolyn completed the round of protests. 'The waves are big. They're dumpers. It looks dangerous and it'll be freezing.'

But Peter was already on his way, running towards the water, splashing into the icy waves to knee height and diving. He swam several metres and lay on his back allowing the waves to roll him where they would, lifting him in their surge of foam and dropping him, propelling him forward towards the shore, and dragging him out as the waves receded. Lying on his back, he could see the sky above him, vast, the bullying clouds forming, great wads of puffed-up white, floating away and reforming.

It was cold but he welcomed it, losing himself in the water, hearing its roar, tasting its saltiness, feeling it entering him. It was elemental. Earth, sky and sea. He was part of its rhythms, allowing them to do with him what they would. They were his masters.

Ellie, Carolyn and Claire were standing at the water's edge, calling. Ellie had waded into the water soaking her jeans below the knee. She was holding a towel stretched out ready in front of her. The girls were watching silently, having hurried to the water's edge, anxious for his health and his safety. Claire was holding his clothes.

As Peter came out of the surf, water streaming from his hair, feeling the glow from his communion with the natural world, and smiling as he walked briskly towards her, Ellie nodded, wrapping him in the towel. She understood.

The day before they returned home, Peter took Ellie to a jeweller on the main street of Avoca, having told the girls he'd like to make the visit alone with his wife. He'd been there with Ellie twice before, a small family business that only sold quality pieces with authentic stones.

Ellie could read Peter's intention. Why else would he have suggested they go without the others. Even Oliver's enthusiasm to come had been trumped by Mrs Blythe.

'Peter, if you're thinking what I think you are…there's no need,' and when she saw his face, 'well, perhaps something very small. Let's see if there's something we both like.'

'How do you know what I'm thinking, Mrs Allthorpe.' Peter was in high spirits.

Ellie was concerned. She knew Peter wanted – no, he needed – to make this gesture, to give her a keepsake, something tangible beyond the love he expressed every day. Such a gift would give her pleasure, but with the sentiment there would be sadness. It would be a reminder, a remembrance, a gift given, not in the carefree years of robust health, but at a time of, well, a time of…

'Here, Ellie, come and look at this.' Peter was excited.

It was a gold ring with a sapphire stone surrounded by diamonds.

'It's beautiful, Peter,' Ellie said.

Peter called to the salesgirl to fetch the ring for Ellie to slip on her finger. It was a perfect fit.

'I hope you're not thinking, Peter… Of course I love it, but it's too much. The cabinet over there has some lovely things at a reasonable price, earrings, rings, pendants…a small token, something small would be nice.'

For Ellie, if he'd chosen a coloured stone from the beach like one of those Oliver had found, it would have lifelong sentimental value. She felt such love for him. At moments like these, he was like an excited little boy.

He bought the ring.

Frank

I like the nurses, most of them. I think they do care. My favourite is Dawn, even though she called me a cranky old bugger, just like that – and you, Frank, she said standing by the bed taking my pulse, are a cranky old bugger. I roared with laughter.

And I like Narelle, though I don't think she likes me. She's young… so timid and innocent, I tease her, can't help myself, ask her what she does with her boyfriend, that sort of thing. You are being rude, Mr Shand, she says in her sweet little voice.

It's all right here now, better than it was. But when I first came in after the accident, and they started doing things to my leg, the pain, never known anything like it. Hell of a night that first one, because one of them doctors, a dopey ignorant young bloke, probably still at medical school, or normal school more like it, said I might lose the leg. I was lucky, but it was smashed up pretty bad. So they set it. Is that what they say when it's been broken, set it, plaster it halfway up the thigh? And the itch you can't reach!

Met Carruthers the next day. He's older, wiry little bloke, seemed to be the main one. He was all right, asked me all these questions. I don't know what most of them had to do with the accident, or even what I was feeling, but he was nodding like one of them clowns at the fun park, the ones with open mouths you put balls in, so it must have been telling him something.

Then there was three of them standing around the bed, with me the prize exhibit. They were looking at scans, chattering away and pointing. Want to tell me what's going on, I ask. It is my body you're talking about, isn't it. They ignore me. I gave Carruthers a bit of lip about that later.

Anyway, one of them bends down and starts prodding and poking my belly, looking up every so often to say something to the others. I tried to hear it but couldn't.

Carruthers tells me later that it might not just be my leg that got smashed up in the accident. There could be something wrong inside. That's what all the poking was about. So they'd like to do some tests. Do what you have to, I said.

Then the physio comes in, big woman with muscular legs and wrestler's arms. She says I'll start walking tomorrow, on crutches. She'll be there to help me. Like hell! But I'm not ready I tell her. To tell the truth, I'm enjoying lying in bed, having me meals brought, though they aren't much to write home about. I could do with a good steak and a beer.

I still curse that woman in the BMW. Built like a tank it was. The car, not her. Didn't even see it coming. Bang, and the sound of broken glass and smashed metal. The pain came a few seconds later. My car written off, hers smashed at the front but she can at least drive it another day.

Then, the bloody hide of the woman, she gets out of the car, dressed in these fancy clothes, black stockings and high heels, Crown jewels around her neck, smelling of roses, fresh from some la-di-da high society lunch, and swear, I've never heard anything like it, ranting and raving, a few words I didn't know. I'll have to ask the fellows down the pub.

She might at least have asked how I was, trapped in the seat with my leg smashed up, and blood on my face. But wait, it gets better. It was your fault, she screams.

My fault, my fault! She can't be serious. She drives straight into me, injures me bad, and says it's my fault. So I give her some lip back. Ask her who the hell she thinks she is, queen of Carlingford?

People come to help. Not her. Might get blood on her fancy clothes. Police come, an ambulance too, and the paramedics free me and take me away. I don't know what happened to her, but I know I haven't heard the end of it. It's all in the hands of the police now. I suppose they took blood here at the hospital. Lucky I hadn't touched a drop. I just hope they tested her too.

I've had a visitor. Pete Allthorpe, the bloke next door with the nice wife. There's a little kid staying with them, kid I helped with advice. Anyway, Pete brought a big basket of fruit and some brownies his wife made, pulled up a chair and sat at the side of the bed.

We talk for a while, the usual stuff starting with how I am, what happened with the accident, what they're doing for me, whether I'm comfortable, whether the hospital food is as bad as people say it is, whether there's anything I need. No, I tell him, there's no one he need contact, but I ask him if he'd mind watering the flowers round the back. I'd just remembered them. They might be dead now.

He tells me a bit about the kid, offers to bring some of my clothes if I tell him where I hide the key. He knows no one else will offer. But I don't want him inside my place.

Then he bowls me over. Can I ask you a personal question, Frank, he says. I don't care if it's personal, they're all the same to me, I tell him. Ask away.

You've been badly hurt, Frank. I imagine it would be true to say you were faced with the possibility of dying. You've been here, in hospital for several days now… He's looking really serious as he's saying all this and I wonder what's coming next. What has the experience taught you, he fires at me. What have you learned from it?

Not to trust bloody women drivers, I answer. No, he says, I mean what have you learned about yourself, has it changed how you think in any way? Changed how I think, I repeat his words because I don't know what he's getting at.

Then he asks me if it's made me think about the purpose of my life. Purpose? You live, you die, you enjoy yourself in between. You try and be nice. Do unto others, that sort of thing. Is that what he was after? I've had an OK time. A good life. I never stole. But if there was anything there to take, I took it. I only had a few small scraps over the years, less than me mates, but as I said to the kid, don't take a backward step. I didn't. But I don't say anything to Pete. I wait for him to say something more.

But he's quiet for a while. We both are. He's thinking. Then he says sorry, Frank, I might have come on a bit heavy. You sure did, brother, I think to myself, but I don't say so.

Well, make sure you do the physio, he says. And be nice to Narelle. I'll come again. Enjoy the fruit, Frank.

Claire

'How's it all going, Dad?' Claire found him in the study reordering his library.

He'd always been organised, with a passion for being neat, but since his news, as the family now called it, order and neatness had become a mania, as if it were on a spectrum with the importance of the law and decent behaviour. The need to set things right.

'Come in, Claire, come in,' and he hurried to join her on the settee. Carolyn was the more frequent visitor of the two girls. He and Ellie had always seen Claire as the less demonstrative of the two, certainly more practical and possibly less emotionally dependent, but you couldn't assess emotion by how visible it was. Still waters run deep.

Claire had sometimes been shushed for being too direct in what she had to say, guilty of a gaffe among family or friends, but it was that very directness that Peter needed now. No sidestepping or averted eyes. No cloaking the truth. He was pleased she'd come to him.

'It's going well,' he answered. 'The strange thing, Claire, is that I feel so well, except for the tiredness and not feeling a hundred per cent after the chemo. The important thing was to get things right, not leave any loose ends, make provision for those I love, and I think I've done that.'

'So you're not hiding anything from us?'

Peter hadn't noticed before, but she had Ellie's eyes, their discerning look, and they were watching him closely.

'No, nothing. None of those side-effects, if that's what you mean. And I have told you everything Chang's told me.'

'And are you afraid, Dad?'

Their hands joined. She leant against him. Peter felt his heart lurch.

'Not so much of death. But I suppose I am afraid of dying. It's not so much the pain, or becoming completely dependent on others, it's turning into someone different, someone not very pleasant. Does that make sense?'

'Yes, I know exactly what you mean. Sean's mother was a lovely woman, always thinking of others and trying to please. When she got sick with the dementia, she became angry, nasty and selfish. She was a different person. But that's not going to happen to you.'

'I hope you're right, Claire.' Peter was enjoying their time together. 'I want to be remembered for who I am, the real me, whoever that is. And I only hope I still have my wits about me. I want to depart this life with dignity.'

They were talking honestly with no attempt to sugar-coat the truth. It was so typical of Claire.

'The real you is impressive, someone we all love.'

'Claire, you mentioned Sean.'

Peter was moved and changed the subject. Family and friends had not pushed Claire for answers when her engagement had been broken suddenly eight years ago. Ellie and Peter had often wondered what happened, but had decided to be there as support, believing she'd talk when she needed to. She hadn't at the time, and she hadn't since. He wondered if she had that need now.

'The reason I don't like talking about it, or didn't all those years ago,' Claire began, aware of Peter's unspoken question, 'is that the whole story is a cliché.'

'How so?' Peter asked.

'The cheating lover, the bride left at the altar, that sort of thing. I felt foolish. I was foolish.'

'So did he cheat, or did he just change his mind?'

'He cheated. Had been for months, though he later tried to make out that it was only the once.'

'And you had no idea?'

'I was young and had no experience of life. Too young and too naïve to read the signs. They must have been obvious to others. Almost as soon as it was over, I began to see things more clearly…the excuses, the unexplained absences, even the sweet smell that he said was his after-shave. I remembered the look on his face and could read the transparent lies. Sometimes, you need to get outside something that's going on to fully realise.'

'Then how did you find out?' Peter felt her hand tighten in his, not from the pain of telling her story, but from the pleasure of telling it, their sharing.

'Made a surprise trip to his apartment. I'd lost my sunglasses and thought they might be there. The door wasn't locked and I thought I heard sounds, they might have been voices, so I went in. I found them in bed. She was a big brassy blonde called Eloise with eyes as big as saucers and enormous…' Claire pointed to her breast with her free hand.

Peter smiled.

'It was kind of comic. He rolls over and sits up, as white as the sheet that had slipped aside to reveal all. And Eloise looks at him with surprise and says, "Who is she, baby?"'

'So you marched out of the place?'

'No, I made them a cup of tea.'

'You did what?!'

They both started to laugh, laughing that continued and grew into hysteria, release, laughter they both needed to have.

It was fully a minute before she could speak. Peter was still laughing.

'I was hurt, but only for a little while. No one likes rejection but I realised almost straightaway that I didn't want to marry him. I didn't love him. It was a blessing in disguise.'

'So it's not that you don't want to be married now?'

'Not at all. I'm not the slightest bit bitter, and I haven't become anti-marriage. If the right person came along, perhaps I might, but sometimes I don't think it's for me. It's great for Carolyn. I think it must have been invented for her, but not for me. Life is complicated enough without adding to it. And we must live life as we see fit.'

'Are you happy, Claire?' Peter placed his arm around her shoulder. She leant further against him. The message welcomed intimacy.

'Yes, I'm happy. You might think it's strange, that my life is not what most women want, the husband and children thing, but I have my work, my family and my friends. I don't need someone to make me feel more complete. And Dad,' she paused for effect, 'you do know, don't you, that when you're gone, I'll be here looking after Mum.'

Peter was moved. 'Yes, I know. And that's a comfort to me. You're so unselfish, Claire.'

'No, Dad, I'm not. Possibly the opposite. It's what I want to do. It's what I need to do.'

'Need to?'

'Yes, need to. I'm no martyr, Dad. I'm not the remaining single daughter trapped into looking after her ageing mother. I want to. I need to. This is my life. It's like a calling, something beyond me.'

Peter had never experienced so close a moment with his grown daughter. Feeling tearful, he hugged her and she returned the hug.

'Perhaps we're all called,' he said, 'and some of us don't hear.'

Susan

'Oh, I'm so glad you're here, Susan. Mrs Clancy keeps asking for you.'

'And how is Olive? Still taking her medication?'

'She's a bit of a handful for the young nurses,' Joyce replied. 'You must have the magic touch.'

Joyce Sedgman was the manager of the Brentwood Nursing Home, a small residential care institution for forty old and infirm residents, a stately old double-storeyed home on spacious grounds that had been tastefully renovated and extended. Pleasant, if a little officious, Joyce was a small dark woman with unflagging energy who expected a lot from her staff, and who looked forward to Susan's twice-weekly voluntary visits. Of course, Susan couldn't see all those in care in her two-day week, but those she did see each week were calmed by her coming.

She made her way down the familiar corridor to Room Eleven, the soft sand-coloured lino muting her tread. A near-naked man shuffled past, his penis nested in a bush of limp hair like an unchaste rose. The look of incomprehension was also familiar.

Olive's eyes lit up when Susan entered the room. 'How are you, Olive?' she asked, approaching the chair where Olive sat with a knitted rug over her lap.

'Not too bad, dear, but my back is giving me a lot of trouble. Had trouble sleeping last night.' She squirmed in her chair.

'I'll talk to the nurses, Olive,' Susan said caringly, 'and see if something more can be done for you.'

'It's kind of you, dear,' Olive whispered. 'I wish they all cared as much as you.'

Susan waited for what she knew was to come.

'It's been three weeks since Pam's been. After all I've done for her, it's not much to expect a visit every week from your own daughter. Do you think I'm being unreasonable, dear?' Her lips began to tremble, her eyes water. 'Would you mind giving her a ring for me, Susan, and telling her she should be thinking a little more about her mother.'

'I tell you what, Olive,' Susan wasn't going to be drawn into a family feud, 'I'll ask Mrs Sedgman. You have to remember I'm not an employee here. I'm a volunteer, and it might be against the rules. But I promise I'll do everything I can.'

Olive looked pleased, though Susan had no intention of making that call. She had cheered Olive, and knew it would soon be forgotten, until next time. Pam was a regular visitor anyway. She had made no false promises.

Her next visit was to Mr Abdullah in another wing of the building.

George Abdullah was a swarthy man with a bulldog face and a shiny bald head, his size a tribute to the resident cook. 'And here she is,' he called, propping himself up in bed, 'the woman of my dreams. I'll bet you've missed me,' he said with a grin.

'George, you don't know how much. Not a single day goes by…'

It was three hours before she left the home. She'd seen seven of the patients. All were delighted to see her.

'Thanks,' Joyce called from the foyer. 'Olive was thrilled. Don't know what we'd do without you. See you on Friday.'

Susan made a detour to the shops on her way home. Elizabeth was coming for lunch, and she loved quiche. That would be perfect with a green salad. She'd asked Tony to buy one that morning, and when she phoned leaving the care home to check, discovered he'd forgotten. He'd come home with a few things but not the very one he'd been sent for. That was no surprise.

'How did it go, Mum?' Elizabeth asked, taking the quiche.

The table was set. The salad dressed in a bowl.

Elizabeth was a tall attractive woman in her early forties with startling green eyes, pale lucent skin and waist-length straight hair, yet untroubled by grey.

'It was good. I feel I make a difference,' Susan answered. 'Joyce Sedg-man thinks so. And the funny thing is, I'm as old as some of them.'

'You'd never think so. And how was, now what's his name, George isn't it, the one who keeps making improper suggestions?'

'Still making them,' Susan laughed. 'And me…a woman about to turn seventy.'

They called Tony and sat at the table. Elizabeth cut the quiche and there was silence as they started to eat.

'Talking of you turning seventy,' Elizabeth began, dangling her fork in the air, 'just to let you know how your party is coming along, all the family have accepted… Sofia, I thought at ninety she wouldn't want to be late on a Saturday night, Vera and Charles, and Leslie and Martin with the two brats.'

'Elizabeth!'

'Sorry, Mum, but you know very well they are.'

'Hear, hear,' Tony contributed, a spare bright-eyed man, his cheeks swelling with quiche.

'And we heard today from the Aubussons. They're coming. We al-ready knew about the Dells, so your old work colleagues will be well represented.'

'I really don't want all this fuss.' Elizabeth was uneasy. 'I feel em-barrassed when the attention is pointed at me. I think I'm more of an observer.'

'Nonsense,' Elizabeth replied. 'It's a special birthday. You didn't have a sixtieth, or a fiftieth, and think of what you did for Tony's birthday, and for Owen and me as kids.'

'Quite right,' Tony agreed. 'Let people do something for you for a change.'

'We'll open the double doors so people can spill out onto the patio,' Elizabeth continued. 'Owen's watching the forecast and if it looks like rain, he's going to hire a huge tent sort of thing. People can dance. He's organised the catering with an old schoolmate, so you won't have to do anything, Mum.'

Elizabeth was becoming more voluble as the plans were revealed. She had taken on the organising with gusto. 'We'll work out where to put the tables for supper, and dad and Owen can set them up. And Dad, it's your job to get the balloons and blow them up… I'll remind you the day before.'

'I don't need reminding.' Tony was defensive.

Elizabeth looked at Susan and smiled.

Lunch was over.

'Tomorrow starts at nine,' Elizabeth said as they took their plates to the sink.

Susan nodded.

Tony looked surprised. 'Tomorrow?' he queried.

'Grandparents' Day at the school, Dad. I did tell you about it and reminded you yesterday. You are coming, aren't you? William and Toby are looking forward to showing you to their teachers and their mates.'

Tony did go, feeling out of sorts. His own schooldays had not been happy, but his spirits lifted when they were greeted at the gates by a welcoming trio of very polite sixth class girls.

The assembly hall was packed with grandparents as the principal welcomed them, praising them for their contribution to the generations that followed, their legacy. Tony seemed bored. Elizabeth was looking forward to the classroom visits, and had already begun chatting with others.

Susan went to William's classroom first. She wasn't sure where Tony had gone.

'Granny,' an excited voice from across the room greeted her.

She was smiling as she threaded her way to his desk, and knelt beside him. The teacher had given the children a worksheet to complete. It was a list of unfinished sentences about their family, and the grandparents were invited to help their charge finish it.

'What I like about my grandpa is…' Elizabeth read, kneeling on the floor next to William's desk. The next line was about her.

'What will we put here, William?' she asked.

He looked at her inquiringly. 'He's nice,' William said, looking for approval.

'Put it down then. Let's see how well you can write.' She could hear the children nearby answering the same question for their grandfathers: 'he plays games with me', 'he's funny', 'he gives me chocolates', 'he loves me'.

She looked around the room. How different it all was now. It was a big room with a reading corner and a small library, and another section of the room had desk computers. She had to stoop beneath the mobiles and the children's artwork pegged on string. A panoply of richly laminated aids covered the walls. The floor was carpeted.

She thought of her early schooldays and the house in Epping, the peanut butter or cold sausage sandwiches her mother never failed to make, ready in her school bag often with a small treat, the trips to and from school with her little brother. Every one of the adults here, she thought, would probably be experiencing the same nostalgia.

On the following Wednesday morning, after Elizabeth had dropped the children at school, she met Susan in town for a ten o'clock fitness class run by Fern, a super fit thirty-year-old blonde in a pink T-shirt and a body-hugging leotard that fitted like a skin.

'You could come too, Dad,' Elizabeth told him. 'There are a couple of men.'

'And Fern's something to look at,' Susan added with a smile.

'No way. They're nearly all women. I'm not going to make a spectacle of myself.'

Vigorous movement was synchronised to loud music, and Fern stood at the front of the room, her back turned, so the class could copy the moves. It was strenuous and hard work for Susan, who had gained a little weight, and wasn't as limber as she had once been. She didn't let on to Elizabeth how much it exhausted her. But she was determined to master the moves, and to fight the problems that came with the onslaught of age.

There was a spread of ages in the group. Most of the women were in their forties, wanting to lose weight or tone their bodies after child-rearing and their children were at school. There was one woman in her late eighties.

This day was the beginning of a new term, and although most of the women were familiar faces, Fern began by thanking them for returning, and made special reference to their only mother and daughter pair. All eyes turned their way. There was polite clapping.

*

Susan decided on a long dress for the party, the navy chiffon she'd worn to Elizabeth's wedding nearly a decade ago. Elizabeth said it was too formal. This was to be smart casual, so Susan wore a black, knee-length tailored skirt and cream blouse. She'd had her hair cut and coloured.

The family arrived together. Sofia took the best armchair and gave orders all night. The brats were taken to a room at the back of the house where they watched an horrific video, emerging noisily only when supper was called.

Susan's work friends arrived politely late, and after introductions talked among themselves. Owen and Elizabeth poured drinks that were consumed so fast they were never free to move around and talk to the guests themselves. Women listened to men talk with fake and arty interest, shifting the weight on their high-heeled feet. Champagne glasses dangled from impatient fingers.

The weather was fine. Stars blazed in the sky, and the guests spilled onto the patio outside.

The caterers moved around offering silver trays of mini sausage rolls, prawns and salmon on crackers, spinach and feta triangles, and lamb kofta.

Susan moved between her guests with a few words of inquiry for them all, doing her best to spark interaction between the family and her friends. Her enjoyment of the occasion was tempered by a concern for them both.

As the music was played at a deafening volume, Elizabeth pulled her husband onto the patio to dance, hoping others would follow.

Owen danced with his mother. 'How's it going, Mum?' he asked.

'I think it's going well, don't you?' she answered, finding it hard to hear.

Owen had done so much towards the evening, she didn't want to tell him that it was hard for her to relax, that she was concerned for her guests who were still talking idly among themselves. And she didn't want to tell him that some soft and dreamy music would be more to their liking, herself included.

Martin, the father of the two boys at the back of the house, cut in, and began to dance with Susan. He was already drunk, his breath stank, and the hand that circled her waist kept sliding down to her bottom where it stayed till she deftly raised it.

'It's the modern way, Susan,' Eric, one of her close friends from work commented about the music, rescuing her from Martin. 'I've asked Owen, he's your son, isn't he, to find something slow and turn the volume down, so I can dance with you.'

Susan was grateful. She'd always liked Eric.

There were some grating noises and something slow began to play.

'Shall we, Mrs Bartoli,' he asked, taking her hand.

'We shall, Mr Simpson,' she answered.

Other couples joined them immediately on the dance floor. The evening had been salvaged.

Supper was served. The guests gathered around the table ladling four different hot dishes and a variety of salads onto their plates, retreating to eat with their plates on their laps. Chairs had been placed outside in clusters on the lawn. Susan was enjoying herself now, and allowed Elizabeth to fill her a plate and bring it to where she was sitting with Owen, Tony and Eric. Family and friends were mingling.

A cake covered in marzipan was wheeled into the family room on a silver trolley. Seven candles adorned it, one for each decade. The usual jokes were made about the difficulty of having seventy candles.

It was time for the formalities, and people made their way inside. Plates were brought with them or left beside chairs on the lawn. Half-eaten nibbles that hadn't passed someone's taste test would be found the following day behind framed pictures on the sideboard, or in flowerpots. The table was covered with near-empty serving dishes. Crumpled serviettes littered the table like muddied flowers.

'Happy Birthday' was sung. The snuffing of seven candles needed no second puff. It was time for the speeches.

Tony hadn't prepared and was uncomfortable with speaking in public. 'Susan's been a wonderful wife, and, er, a wonderful mother to Elizabeth and Owen.' A long pause followed. 'She's always been there for us, and um, put us first, well, most of the time.' He paused for a reaction, thinking it might be amusing. There was none.

'Give it to me. It's mine,' was heard from the back room.

'Well,' Tony concluded, 'happy birthday, love, may there be many more, and thank you all for coming.'

Elizabeth and Owen had prepared their speeches to complement each other, and were glowing in praise of their mother.

It was Susan's turn. She was emotional but spoke well, talking of the importance of friends and family, paying tribute to Tony and her children, and providing some home-spun philosophy about ageing. She ended with a statement about the need for everyone to look out for each other in these troubled times. There was generous applause.

The guests left together in the early hours of the morning. Sofia was fast asleep and had to be wakened, but swore she'd never slept a wink. The brats had found a new lease of life.

'We'll clean up in the morning,' Elizabeth said.

'Not you, Mum,' Elizabeth replied. 'That's our job.'

*

After a long examination of herself in the mirror to determine if the magical seventy had left an indelible mark, Susan lay in bed with Tony discussing the party. She was pleased with how it had gone and warmed by the compliments she'd received.

'I think it went well,' she said, anxious for Tony to share her opinion. 'After a while, people started to get on together, my friends and the family, particularly when they turned the music down and the dancing started. Thank you again Tony. And Elizabeth and Owen were terrific. I'm very lucky.'

'The family certainly enjoyed it,' Tony replied yawning, 'though I'm not sure how long Sofia was part of the action.' He laughed.

'Your family, Tony.'

'Pardon.'

'I said your family. Your family, they enjoyed it.'

'It's your family too, Susan.' There was an awkward pause. 'It's a pity some of your own family, if that's the point you're making, couldn't have been here.'

'There aren't any.'

'What about that brother you were always talking about? What was his name?'

'Peter.'

'Yes, Peter. You never thought of getting in touch with Peter?'

'Often.'

'Then…'

'There was one birthday, I must have been about fourteen. That would make him about eleven. He was late home from school, said he had to see someone. I thought he was up to something because we used to walk home together. There was a knock on my door when I was doing my homework, and he comes in hiding something behind his back. It was a big bunch of flowers, not from someone's garden, but from a florist. They were beautiful. I found out later he'd spent every cent of his pocket money. I can still see his face…it was radiant. He was so proud handing me the flowers.'

'You can still…'

'I don't even know if he's alive.'

'Susan.' Tony was becoming impatient. 'It's still not too late to get in touch with…what's his name?'

'It's Peter, Tony! Peter!'

Peter

'I start tomorrow, Ellie. I'm going to look for Susan.'

They were undressing for bed. These were the times before they rolled over to sleep that were often the most fertile for hatching new plans, sharing insights or simply taking stock. It hadn't escaped Ellie's attention that Peter had been quiet at dinner, obviously deep in thought. Once, she'd asked him a question and didn't get an answer.

'That's wonderful,' she replied.

About time, she thought, but didn't say so. It had always puzzled her that he hadn't tried to find Susan, and had decided it was best not to push him too hard to do so. Lack of interest on his part didn't seem to be a satisfactory answer. There could be some other reason, one that might be painful to resurrect.

'I'm not getting my hopes up. She might have died. She was older than me. And she mightn't want to see me.'

'This might sound sexist, Peter, but I can't imagine a woman, particularly a grown woman, not wanting to see her brother after all this time, unless something terrible…'

'I hope you're right, El.'

It was obvious Peter didn't want to talk about reasons now. Probably, Ellie thought, because apathy was the least acceptable of them.

'So this is about, what did you call it, your quiet completeness?' Ellie was slipping her nightie over her head.

'You think that's strange?' Peter was looking at her questioningly as she stood beside the bed, but could see that she was serious.

'No, no, I wasn't making light of it. I wasn't teasing you. I think I said at the time I understood, that I'd feel the same.'

'Let's say then that it's my need to see a lucid life.'

'I understand completely,' Ellie replied, and moved around the bed to hold him. It was important he knew she gave him her full support.

Peter retired to his study after an early breakfast. His cup of coffee was still half full, the second slice of toast still in the toaster. Most of his search could be done online. Ellie smiled at Claire who smiled back and gave a thumbs-up.

His first step was to search the *White Pages*. There was a website he could use to search an Australia-wide directory. He found nine entries for S. Allthorpe in Australia. Five were in New South Wales. There was no knowing if they were Susan. They could be Sally, Stella, Scott or Steven. Gender wasn't given. It was a long shot, but it was a start. He recorded the phone numbers. That would not be too big a task to ring them all later. At least her name wasn't 'Smith'.

Only when he'd finished did another disturbing thought occur to him. She might not be in Australia at all. If she'd been so desperate to get away all those years ago, she might have left the country, or gone any time in the last fifty years.

His second step was to search the electoral rolls stored in the Australian Electoral Commission. After an exhaustive search, he was able to locate the five entries for S. Allthorpe in New South Wales. Three were women, and there wasn't a Susan but a Susannah. He recorded the information he needed to contact her, and explained his progress to Ellie over lunch.

'But why would S. Allthorpe change Susan to Susannah? That doesn't make sense. If I wanted to change my name, I'd make it something altogether different like Amity or Ursula. I don't think it's her, Peter.'

'I don't think it is either,' Peter agreed, needing a second opinion. It was early days and he wasn't about to give up yet. He was enjoying the hunt, it was something he needed to do, and knew he should have done long ago. He realised his search so far assumed her name hadn't changed. Still, it was a start. 'She was an attractive girl, and she would almost certainly have married. She often spoke of having children.'

'My understanding, Peter, is that you don't need a formal change of name, but Births, Deaths and Marriages issues a marriage certificate you need for things like driving licences and passports.'

'That's helpful, Ellie.'

So after lunch, Peter retired to his study again, momentarily disturbed by the mention of death, and started the third stage of his search. Births Deaths and Marriages, entered in the website as BDM, also allowed a search of name changes.

Ellie was in the kitchen preparing dinner when Peter joined her late in the afternoon. 'How's it going, darling?' she asked, cutting onions. 'Getting anywhere?'

'Making progress,' he answered in a subdued voice, taking a piece of paper from his shirt pocket.

'What's that?' Ellie asked as expected.

'That,' said Peter more forcefully, waving the paper in the air, and becoming more animated, 'shows the contact details of a Susan Bartoli who used to be Susan Allthorpe.'

'Peter!' She rushed to him, still holding a saucepan. 'It's her? You found her! Where is she?'

It was so like him to make out that it was nothing much when it was momentous, even for him. Reminiscent of his front of nonchalance when visiting Enright. He was obviously pleased.

'We've found an aunt for you, Claire,' Ellie told her when she arrived home minutes later. 'I've already told Carolyn and they're coming to dinner…a celebration.'

'Susan. You've found Susan?' Claire was as excited as Ellie.

'All these years, and it only took…' She didn't see Ellie shaking her head, warning her not to continue.

Over dinner, they discussed how Peter should make contact. 'I can hardly knock on the front door and say, "Hello, Susan, long time no see."'

'Obviously you phone first, make a time,' Claire said, 'then you can knock on her door and say, 'Long time no see.''

They were all enjoying themselves.

'Where's Braidwood?' Ellie asked.

'I think it's a little this side of Canberra…two and a half, three hours' drive at the most. I could come with you, but I think it's better that you go alone.'

*

He'd never made a phone call like this. He asked Ellie and Claire if he could make it alone, and closed the study door. He would let them know as soon as he had any news. They understood. It was deeply personal.

For several minutes, he sat at his desk, staring at the wall opposite, where a gibbous moon was shining through the branches of the pittosporum leaving a scribbling on the wall. He could hear crickets outside. Inside, the house was silent.

Once more, he couldn't find words for his feeling. A numb feeling, a bit like that he'd felt in Enright's rooms, but not one of dread, more one of awe, a feeling that he was venturing into the unknown, that things might never be the same again.

Would anyone be home? Might they have moved in the last year or month? If she answered, would he recognise her voice? Would she recognise his?

He could still remember her voice, its musical quality, how soothing it was, the upward inflection at the end of a sentence when she was excited…and the smile that came with it, infecting its sound with pleasure. Of course it might be very different now, coarsened by the years. Her indifference would be hard to bear, but he kept telling himself that even her indifference would in some way satisfy his need to have tried, to stamp his life with a quiet completeness.

His fingers were putty as he pressed the buttons on his mobile phone. He was shaking, entered the wrong number, too many digits, and had to do it again. He leant forward, resting his elbows on the desk to support his hands. Had he called the right number this time? And then the count down, a slow ringing, once, twice, three times, four, and finally a man's voice.

'Hello.'

Was this to be it? The moment of truth.

He took a breath. 'May I speak to Mrs Susan Bartoli, please?'

Silence for a second as if the man was considering whether to oblige, or whether to ask his name, his reason for calling, and then, thankfully, 'Hang on, I'll get her.'

Relief of sorts. He'd hoped, prayed she'd answer. A man, probably her husband had done so, but thankfully he didn't ask who was calling. Peter didn't want to give his name, to have his identity revealed to her in some offhand way by someone else, as though he were just another telemarketer.

'For you, Susan,' he heard the man say.

'Who is it?' A woman's voice, a long way off, was too distant to recognise.

'Don't know.'

Several seconds of pregnant silence. Did he imagine footsteps?

'Hello. Susan Bartoli speaking.'

Peter knew. It was the voice he remembered, the voice that had counselled and soothed him all those years ago. A little older, perhaps with a little less music, but there was no mistaking it. He could feel his heart pounding.

'Hello,' she said again.

'Susan,' he answered. 'It's Peter, your brother.'

A few seconds of silence. Time stopped.

'Peter, Peter, is it really you? Peter, oh my God, Peter.' She was crying. 'I'd know your voice anywhere. You won't believe how often I've thought about…how are you…where are you…are you well, happy? You can't know how much this means…'

'What's the matter?' The man's voice in the background was alarmed. 'Has he upset you?'

'It's Peter, Peter, my brother Peter.'

Susan and Peter

Winter and a constipated sun peered through rags of cloud. A frost was melting on the lawn. The Federal Highway to Canberra was easy driving, and Peter had left early.

'You'll be there hours before time, Dad,' Claire said.

'I'll take my time,' he replied, 'stop along the way, get a coffee, go and look at the antiques at Berrima.'

Ellie and Claire could see his excitement and anxiety, and were even more attentive than usual. They were concerned that his medical condition might pose problems with such a long return trip.

He relaxed on the drive, trying, as he often did, to put what he felt into words so the very words might anchor his thoughts and feelings, make them intelligible, captured and named. He felt that it all wasn't really happening, that it was somewhere outside him. The paradox that he might be beginning a new life when another was ending, and in a very real sense.

He drove in silence, well under the speed limit, strangely aware of the trees, the flat expanses of land and the bone-coloured sky with its drifting clouds. The thought of meeting her brought back memories.

The boys were jeering.

'You're chicken, Allthorpe,' Gleeson the class bully called, with a nasty sneer.

'You're a sissy,' his offsider said.

His face was flaming with embarrassment. They were looking up at the big dipper at Luna Park. He was seven. So were they, but they weren't going on the ride.

'Afraid you'll puke, Allthorpe?'

'Come on, Peter,' Susan said softly so the other boys couldn't hear, 'we'll do it together.' She was only ten as she took his hand and they walked bravely to join the small queue to the big dipper. Gleeson's taunts died on his lips.

Goulburn. As Claire said, he would be too early, so he found a parking spot in the main street, walked around a block of shops and entered a small café. He sat in a booth with vinyl-padded olive seats along one wall. Poor-quality artwork from local artists was on sale and hanging on the opposite wall. A large woman with fat arms was making sandwiches behind the counter. He was joined immediately by the waitress.

She was probably fifteen or sixteen, wore a very short black skirt, and even in winter, a sleeveless blouse that exposed tattooed arms. 'What'll it be?' she said pleasantly, her notepad ready, the silver stud gleaming on her tongue.

He drank his coffee and returned to the car, wondering what she thought of him, if she thought anything at all, a conservative and probably unfashionable older man. He recalled how they used to be called fuddy-duddies. He mused at how times had changed, the perennial lament of those who lose their youth. Am I a fuddy-duddy, he wondered.

He liked the look of Braidwood, but he was still too early so he drove around the streets to get the feel of the place. He imagined her there. Did she go to that supermarket, that church? Did her children, if she had them, once go to that school?

It was something he always did when he met new people or simply saw them at work. He'd already recreated the day of the girl in the café at Goulburn, the hectic pace of lunchtime trade, eating a bagel and sipping a Diet Coke for lunch, and evenings in a littered apartment with raucous music and a boyfriend he reckoned looked a lot like her. And so he'd known the lives of clerks, fishermen and shop attendants everywhere, a fellowship of sense.

From the front, the house seemed to be large. It was triple-fronted, and single-storeyed in truscott brick, on a flat block of land. There was a rose garden against the fence and a garden seat. Susan had always liked roses. He parked the car outside and got out, thinking he should have brought something, but what? Flowers or chocolates didn't seem appropriate yet, and he hadn't been invited for a meal, so wine was out of the question. What was the protocol for meeting a family member after fifty years?

It all seemed unreal as he began the short walk up a gravel drive from the front gate. Aware of the thump of his heart, he thought he saw a flicker of movement behind the curtain in the front window.

*

She'd been up for hours, hadn't slept well. Elizabeth and Owen had called before they left for work to wish her well, both warning her about expecting too much. 'Time can play some nasty tricks,' Owen had said. Tony was dismissed with a kiss.

'I'd like to be here by myself,' she'd told Tony the night before. 'It's your morning at the club anyway.'

Elizabeth and Owen had been warned not to call or make a surprise visit.

Susan had been overwhelmed by the phone call. It was strange because after the party, she had decided to look for Peter. It may have been a week or two before she started to do so, but that coincidence must surely be weird after more than half a century.

When she'd heard the words, 'Susan, it's Peter, your brother', she recognised the voice and was stunned. It was more mature but unmistakable. She found it hard to hold onto the phone. For a second, she wondered if it was a friendly call, but she soon felt his relief. And her own reaction must have left no doubt for him about her own excitement.

When she finally had the house to herself, an hour before Peter was due, she checked on her black slacks and cream crocheted top that had been laid flat on the bed. She would put them on just before he arrived. And just a little make-up. She wanted to look her best.

She sat on the bed, thinking of the house in Epping, thinking of how her life had shaped itself since, wondering if she had done the shaping or something outside her had done it, thinking of that night, the night that was to change her life.

She'd packed a small overnight bag the evening before. One change of clothes, underwear and toiletries. She'd taken the overnight bag from her mother's closet and hid it under her bed. She only had a small amount of money, a few notes and coin in her jeans pocket. She knew where her mother kept the housekeeping money, but she wasn't going to take it. She hadn't given much thought to where she'd go or what lay ahead.

It was black in her room and dark outside. Perhaps she was lucky that there was no moon. She sat on her bed, still neatly made, wearing her jeans, sloppy-joe and track shoes, still wondering if she was doing the right thing. But she'd made the decision long before, and she wasn't going to change her mind now. She had to go.

She'd been to her bedroom door twice already, opening it ajar to check. Each time, there was a murmur of voices and a light was still on, so she returned to her bed to wait.

The third time, a long time later, it was dark, and there was no sound coming from her mother's bedroom next to her own. She opened her door, closing it after her without a sound, and stood still in the hallway holding her bag. She could hear a faint snoring, then silence and a creak. Was someone walking around? She froze and waited. What explanation could she give for standing there stock-still with a bag? But there was no other sound. It must have been the house settling.

She crept along the hall to her brother's room. The door was open, and she could see him lying on his back with the doona pulled to his chin. He looked angelic, the shock of blond hair lapping his forehead, so trusting, and she was leaving him.

For a moment she hesitated, emotional, but she had to go. She couldn't tell him. He would have been too upset, and would have wanted to go with her. He might have aroused suspicion in their mother. And she was in no position to take him with her. How could a young teenage girl look after an even younger brother?

A step at a time, carefully opening the front door and closing it. No lights came on. A last look at the house, then silently into the black night that swallowed her, pulling down the sleeves of her sloppy-joe to cover her freezing fingers, walking carefully to avoid treading on twigs or gravel until she was well down the road.

The rest was a wash of memory, her friend's apartment on the other side of the city that was given free for a fortnight, the lowly paid job stocking shelves in a supermarket, the homesickness, the propositions from customers and landlords, the struggling to make ends meet, the trip with a work mate to Braidwood, and Tony.

She looked at her watch. Not long now. She put on her clothes, imagining where he might be this instant, took one final look at herself in the mirror, and went into the family room. He'd been a boy who'd always made sure he was on time. She wondered if he'd changed.

He hadn't. There was the sound of a car stopping outside. She went nervously to the window, moving the curtain aside a fraction to look. An athletic-looking older man was closing the car door behind him. She couldn't see his face but it had to be him. He looked up at the house, and seemed to be looking straight at her. Embarrassed, she let the curtain fall, and went to the door.

*

'Peter.'

'Susan.'

They were in each other's arms, not with fierce emotion, but with an intuitive and instant understanding, the surety of surviving and enduring love. It wasn't planned. It just happened. They stayed that way for a minute, saying nothing. Perhaps anything would have seemed trite.

Then she held him at arm's length. 'You look wonderful, Peter. You haven't changed. Just a slightly older version of little brother.' Her voice was trembling. 'I saw you walking from the car and could tell you work at keeping fit. It's only the baldness…' And she laughed. 'But what man of nearly seventy hasn't lost hair?'

Peter raised his hand to feel his scalp and gave a start. He should have worn his cap. Then he held her at arm's length. His turn. 'I won't say you haven't changed. You've kept your figure, you look good, the hair might be greyer, but the smile's the same.'

'Don't flatter me, little brother. I don't think this is the figure I had over fifty years ago.' She laughed again and led him into the family room, where they sat watching and holding each other, talking of their families, giving a potted history of their lives for the last half-century.

'I've prepared lunch, Peter,' she said two hours later, 'but no marshmallows. Remember how you loved them, with grated nuts on ice cream. It's nothing extravagant.' But it was, a pineapple beef casserole and potato bake.

'I didn't ask on the phone, Peter, but we're all hoping you'll stay the night. It's a shame to have to drive back the same day. You can have the spare bedroom. From what you've told me about Ellie, I'm sure she wouldn't mind. Please say yes. I could talk to Ellie if you like. Tony will be home soon and Elizabeth and Owen want to meet you.'

They talked throughout the afternoon reliving old times.

Tony arrived home and was gracious. 'I can see the family likeness,' he said, and chatted for a while before changing his clothes and going to his workshop at the back of the garage. He knew when to be scarce.

Dinner was a merry affair with Peter and Susan competing in telling stories about their life together as children. Elizabeth had arrived and rushed into the room to hug 'my uncle Peter'. Owen had welcomed him warmly with less fanfare.

'Remember the time, Susan, you were still in primary school, and you wanted to impress that ginger-haired boy – Michael, was it? – so you went into Mum's bedroom and used her lipstick. You made your lips enormous…brilliant red, right up to your nostrils, and they covered the width of your face.'

'That's an exaggeration, Peter Allthorpe. I remember the time you went into Dad's study and tried using his fountain pen, but you spilt ink on the open pages of his prize first edition book, can't remember what it was. But what did you do? You carefully cut out about thirty damaged pages and hid them hoping Dad wouldn't notice.'

'He really did that?' Elizabeth was laughing so much the tears were streaming down her face.

'Wait, there's more. Not being too bright, my brother here put them in the rubbish bin, where Dad found them.'

'Not fair, Susan Bartoli. I went to Dad and told him.'

Everyone was happy. Tony laughed and told a few stories of his childhood that not even Susan had heard. The sharing was infectious. Elizabeth and Owen shared a craving for stories of their mother's past. It was something of a mystery to them.

Peter stayed the night. He'd called Ellie in the afternoon, saying he'd be back late the following day, and that everything was going better than he'd hoped. 'She's just as I remembered her,' he told Ellie. 'It's as if we've never been apart.'

'He's great, Mum,' Elizabeth whispered to Susan as she left for home. 'I'm so pleased…for us both. You must be thrilled.'

She was.

The following day, when they were alone together in the house, and Peter was sitting in a lounge chair, Susan moved the other chair so that she could sit down and face him. She took both his hands in her own. 'Peter,' she said softly and paused, looking at him steadily.

Peter could see a faint pink suffuse her cheeks. He'd always known there were more serious things they had to talk about. He'd been about to raise them himself.

'For all these years, I was so worried that you might be mad with me, and never want to see me again.'

Peter was shaking his head vigorously, and opened his mouth to speak, but Susan raised a hand to stop him.

'At first when I left, I thought you wouldn't like me any more. I thought you'd be hurt that I'd gone and hadn't told you. I thought you'd be mad with me and think I didn't care.'

Peter watched her tenderly. This was difficult for her. And for him.

'As the weeks became months and years, I became more and more convinced. And then there was Tony and the children.' She stopped. Her eyes were wet. She wanted his reaction.

'But Susan, why did you think I didn't like you? Why would I be mad with you? You were the most important thing in my life. I'd have done anything for you.'

'I left without telling you, but the real reason was what you saw that terrible night. I was sure you'd never feel the same about me again.'

'Susan, Susan, I know the night you mean. How could I ever forget it? I remember…'

'Please Peter, let me explain. This isn't easy for me.' She gripped both of his hands more firmly, and knelt on the floor in front of him, looking at him intently before continuing. 'You saw me naked on the bed with Paul, not exactly in his arms, but he was lying pressed up against me, half naked himself.'

'Yes, but…'

'No, let me finish. It was the third time our so-called loving stepfather had crept into my room at night. He'd say how important I was, how he felt for me, how it was more than a father to daughter feeling, that ages didn't matter, and he'd take off my clothes, slowly, one thing at a time. I resisted, you have to believe that, told him I didn't want him doing it, that it wasn't right, I was uncomfortable, but he wouldn't listen. I wanted to call out. It was horrible. I hated what he was doing, but I was worried about Mum. I even thought she might blame me. I'd heard some women did that to preserve their marriage. Put their husband first before their children. I kept telling him I wasn't comfortable but he kept wheedling and picking at my clothes until he'd removed all of them, telling me it was all right, that there was nothing wrong with it. And he'd push against me, explore with his hands. I could feel his hardness.'

Susan's eyes were lowered but she still held on to Peter's hands. Her grip tightened even more. She was struggling for composure.

'I looked up, Peter, and there you were standing in the doorway in your pyjamas, staring in disbelief. It must have come as a terrible shock for you. It was for me. Seeing you standing there completely bewildered made me feel even worse about myself, made me feel even more dirty. You were only there for a few seconds. I wanted to call out to you but couldn't. By the time I'd gathered my wits, it was too late. You'd disappeared. I wanted to tell you it wasn't my idea. I didn't want him there, but I was naked with him and I wasn't calling out in protest. So I thought you wouldn't believe me, that you wouldn't believe how awful it was for me. I thought you'd hate me for it.' She was crying softly.

Peter looked stunned, and put his arms around her shoulders, gently pulling her head to his own so their foreheads touched. 'But you left,' he whispered.

'Peter,' she wiped her eyes and blew her nose, 'I wasn't even sixteen. I was ashamed, and I was confused. I worried what you'd think of me. He was hard against me, and each time he tried to go a little bit further. I knew it was the beginning, and I knew enough about life to know where it would end…and soon. And there was Mum to consider. She was the real reason. I needed to get away for her sake. What else could I do?'

'So Susan, you held off contacting me because you felt ashamed, you felt I was disgusted with you?'

Susan nodded. 'That, and the circumstances life fires point-blank at us. I'm sorry, Peter. I truly am. You're as white as a sheet.'

Peter leant forward and lifted her to a standing position. They held each other greedily.

'This is bizarre,' he whispered, still holding her. 'You'll certainly think so too when you hear my side of things.'

'I can't imagine…'

Peter interrupted. His need to explain was as great as hers had been. 'You're right about me standing at the door for a few seconds, and yes, I was in shock. I saw my sister, naked, and this man neither of us particularly liked pressing suggestively against her. I still have the image of his thin pale legs and the curly hairs and blotches on his back.'

Susan's head was resting in his lap as he spoke. He could feel the tickle of her hair.

'Susan, I was twelve, nearly thirteen. I wasn't a little boy any more. I knew what he wanted to do to you. I never thought for a moment that you wanted him. I knew, I could tell by the glimpse I had of your face, that it disgusted you.'

'Thank you, Peter,' she said. 'That does make me feel a little better.' She was obviously relieved. She returned to her seat and held his hands. 'Well, now that we've…'

'No, no,' Peter interrupted. 'There's more, a lot more. While you were being set upon by that man, and I knew what he was up to, what did I do? I'll tell you what I did, Susan. I slunk away like a coward. I went back to my bedroom and pretended nothing was happening.'

'But Peter…'

'At the very least, I could have shouted, I could have come into the room and told him to stop what he was doing. I might even have wrestled with him, or hit him. But I didn't. You're right about the other circumstances in our life, but perhaps we become very good at using them as excuses. Susan, if shame stopped you contacting me, it was guilt that stopped me contacting you.'

*

His trip home was with a lighter heart than when he'd come. He felt a weight had been lifted from his shoulders. Owen had called from his office to say goodbye.

Elizabeth had dashed from her work for a quick lunch with them, and hugged him. 'You're already my favourite uncle,' she'd said.

'And you're my favourite niece,' he replied, returning the hug.

Tony's 'Welcome to the family, Peter' earned him a sidelong glance from Susan.

His farewell to her was emotional.

'It's just like old times,' she said.

They hugged and made promises of seeing each other soon that were more than the departing standards. She stood in the driveway waving until the car was out of sight, missing him already, and walked very slowly back to the house, needing time to herself.

He hadn't told her his news, that it was more than likely he would die within several months, that there was even a possibility he might not see her again if he didn't have that long. He was going to tell her, but their brief time together had brought unexpected pleasure. They were together as loving brother and sister, and they had cleared the air of what had been lying under the surface for both of them, what had put a brake on the feeling that had never gone away. To tell her then would have saddened their newly discovered happiness.

As he drove, he wondered how he would tell her. He didn't want his death to come as a surprise phone call without her knowing that he'd been terminally ill when they'd met. That might undo the honesty and transparency, the opening of their hearts to each other.

Ellie and the girls were waiting eagerly at home for him, so he wouldn't stop at Berrima or Goulburn on the way. They'd want every last detail of what had happened. The girls would want to know all about their long-lost aunt and cousins. How much would he tell them about what happened in the house at Epping half a life ago? How much did they need to know? Wasn't that a secret he shared with Susan?

But he would tell Ellie. He'd tell her everything. She always understood.

Ellie and Peter

'She sounds a lovely person, Peter.' I'm looking forward to meeting her.'

'She is lovely, Ellie. I'm sure you'll feel the same way I do…so strange…after half a century of course we were different…but in some ways it was as if we'd never been apart.'

'I'm glad you told me the whole story, about that awful night. It's finally making sense. It did make me sad, though.'

'Why, El?' Peter could only think of his meeting with Susan, and not what had happened before, or what had been lost.

'How the course of a life can change because of one incident, even a simple misunderstanding. Sometimes it all seems so…' Ellie was searching for a word, 'fragile, I suppose…capricious.'

It was the first night of his return, and they were lying in bed together some time after midnight. It was where they discussed matters of importance before they went to sleep. Ellie had been pleased and relieved when he returned. She thought it likely that he might be met with disappointment. So when he returned in high spirits, she was doubly pleased, pleased that there was a resolution to his half-century of wondering, and happy that the success of his visit would help him cope with the likely outcome of Enright's looming prediction.

'But why didn't you tell me before about that night, and what you saw, and felt? We'd spoken several times about your reluctance to get in touch with her.'

'I've been thinking about that all the way home, El. I wonder if feelings and thoughts are sometimes so vague, so amorphous, they need a word to give them focus, to define them. I was uneasy for all those years but I never identified my feelings as guilt. That would have been too harsh a word then.'

'So what changed?'

'I think it was Susan's revelation. The more she talked, the more she told me about what she had to endure, the clearer it became. It put things in perspective.'

'What exactly?'

'That I was the one at fault.'

'You don't think you're being too harsh on yourself, Peter? You were still a boy, a boy with little understanding and certainly no experience of life.'

'But look at the price she had to pay. Think of the hell she went through. If I'd done something…'

Carolyn and Claire were excited to hear about Susan. They wanted to know everything that happened. They wanted a detailed description of what she looked like, and were disappointed Peter had not thought to take a photo.

'You never even thought about it,' Carolyn marvelled.

They were particularly interested in Elizabeth and Owen, their cousins.

*

The family's buoyant mood changed a few days later when they heard of Frank's death. He'd returned from the hospital and died the following day. It hadn't been expected, at least not as far as they knew, and Ellie had made a casserole and taken it to him that very day. She'd found him, unable to rouse him from his veranda chair. It was a painful reminder of what lay ahead for them.

Peter and Ellie attended the funeral in drizzling rain. Ellie didn't want them to go, and made excuses, saying that even though he lived next door, they'd never been very close. Peter hugged her without saying a word. He knew what she was trying to do, but needed to make this final gesture.

Pristine and Omo-white White Ladies, tasteful with maroon relief, adorned the church, and a few fraying knots of mourners, all people who lived in the same street, thought of washing on the line, and picking children up from school.

'Do mean people go to Heaven?' Oliver asked Peter on the day of the funeral.

Ellie sat leaning against Peter in the church, very aware of the unease of his feelings. She felt them too. He seemed to be looking around, at the altar, the messages in the stained-glass windows, the golden eagle fronting the pulpit, and the vaulted ceilings, trying to glean meaning from them.

He felt moved by a mysterious force. It was, after all, he later told her, the house of God. He needed to see the rhyme and reason of his life in the bigger scheme of things before he kissed the cheek of time. He knew it would not come as a revelation, as something finite, but it was a beginning. It would be a work in progress, learning that would continue until his final hours.

Aware of Ellie's hand holding his, he found himself giving thanks, not just for everything that had been given to him, but for his growing understanding that life and death were part of one design. How awesome it all was. There were so many things he'd taken for granted, little things that he would never feel the same about again….the dew that glistens on a spider's web, the dancing motes in shafts of light, the magpie's song of joy, the jasmine's scent…

He thought of his earlier talks with Frank, and how the thought of what came next, so pressing for him now, neither daunted nor intrigued Frank. There didn't seem to be a question of the purpose for his years, not even a dying vision of the thump of dirt on coffin wood, or the trenchant lettering on a plaque or tombstone. He'd never wondered at the purpose of the universe, or sussed out a notion of his place in it.

The day Enright gave him the news that changed his life, he'd left the hospital alone saying he would make his death the crowning glory of his life. Of course he hoped there'd be other things he'd be remembered for, perhaps other crowning glories, or more modest accomplishments. He remembered it being said of Cawdor in *Macbeth* that nothing in his life became him like the leaving it. He still hoped there'd be some truth in that for him.

Peter and Ellie

'Hello, Peter, Ellie.'

'Hi, Daisy. How did your daughter go in her exams?' They were on first name terms now with the receptionist at Dr Chang's.

Daisy was a Chinese Australian with fine chiselled features and cream-coloured straight hair like that of a doll. Reserved at first, she had become fond of them and welcomed their interest. 'Dr Chang will only be a minute.'

Ellie had been with Peter to each of his four chemo treatments and blood tests. He was capable of driving home, but grateful for the moral and practical support. As soon as she had known Peter's news, she had said it was something they'd share. And they had.

As they waited, sitting in the black chairs that lined two walls of the waiting room, Ellie would help herself to the free coffee, find a piece or two for the two-thousand-piece jigsaw, and chat to Daisy when she wasn't busy. Peter would also have his turn talking to Daisy, provoking her with light-hearted banter.

Dr Chang had called them a few days before Peter's next round of chemo was due to begin and wanted to talk to them. He'd never done that before.

'That's odd,' Ellie had said. 'No need to worry. It's probably standard procedure.'

'I don't think so, Ellie. It can only mean one thing.'

'You're getting ahead of yourself, Peter. There's no reason to think the worst.'

'But why else…'

She moved to the jigsaw table, where the puzzle was more than half finished. Peter selected a magazine reporting broken romances among celebrities. It would normally have made him chuckle, report its gossip to Daisy. Today it didn't.

The door opened framing the lean, antiseptic figure of Dr Chang. He invited both Peter and Ellie to enter. He had become quite close to them both. Over the years, he'd found that his terminal patients coped in different ways. Some remained grim and tight-lipped throughout, some used humour as a defence, and for others, a single sympathetic word led to a deluge of spoken fears. Only a few remained bitter.

Not only were Peter and Ellie sensible in the way they approached Peter's prognosis, they showed an interest in the treatment he provided. They even showed an interest in him. The well-being of a doctor was usually the last thing on a patient's mind.

As they entered, Daisy signalled her good luck with a thumbs-up. There was nothing in her manner to suggest that she knew anything about the reason for the visit. Doctors would never discuss patients with their receptionist.

'Is there something you need to discuss with us, doctor?' Ellie asked before either of them had sat down. She was anxious.

Peter was ill at ease. Chang sat behind his desk holding what must have been a report of findings. The air was heavy with portent.

'I have some shocking news, Peter,' he said.

It's finally come to this, Peter thought. He had half-anticipated a time when tests would reveal his condition was irreversible, or had considerably worsened. It would be a time when the oncologist would say that there was nothing more chemotherapy could do. He might even suggest they discontinue it. That would mean another decision he would have to make.

A second's glance around the room, and nothing had changed. The couch neatly covered in paper towelling, the cupboards, the washbasin, all just as they had always been. The material world remained the same. Indifferent. Only his view of things didn't.

He felt Ellie tense beside him, and her hand reach out to rest on his knee. At least she was with him.

'No, let me rephrase that,' Chang continued. 'I have some extraordinary news.' He paused to savour the moment. 'Sometimes in the medical world, there are things that can't be explained. It isn't an exact science.'

Peter was leaning forward expectantly on the chair. He was ready for the worst. Why was Chang prolonging things? This was torture. How long, was the question uppermost in his mind. Ellie didn't know what to think.

'The cancer's gone,' Chang said suddenly, a smile appearing on his face, a face rarely given to smiling. 'Not a trace,' and he waved the report in the air.

Peter and Ellie were silent for several seconds. Chang waited.

Ellie was the first to react. 'That's, that's wonderful. You're sure, doctor? There couldn't be a mistake, could there?'

Chang was still smiling and shaking his head.

'Peter, oh Peter.' She hugged him as he remained sitting on the chair, then slipped to kneel on the carpet in front of him between his legs so she could put both arms around him. He rested his head on her shoulder.

Peter hadn't moved, hadn't reacted. Sometimes, emotion lags behind knowledge.

'It's over, then,' he eventually managed, still bewildered, the truth slowly gathering momentum.

He'd later admit to being somewhere else in those first few minutes, in some untapped part of his mind that dulled the senses, an anaesthesia of near-comprehension without feeling. But he could hear Chang speaking, as if his voice was coming from a deep-sea chamber.

'Obviously we'll need to see you again, Peter, say in two or three months, just to check,' and he came towards Peter, taking his limp hand in both of his. 'I can't tell you how pleased I am. There aren't that many good luck stories in my line of work.'

'So do I stop treatment…no more medication?' Peter was still finding it hard to believe.

'None.' Chang couldn't hide his pleasure.

Peter and Ellie told an emotional Daisy the news on the way out, and she emerged from behind the counter and hugged them both. 'And don't come back.' Her laughter was mixed with tears.

They went straight home. Ellie drove, her exuberant chatter a contrast to Peter's near-silence. She knew that shock could come from sudden unexpected good as well as sudden bad, but she couldn't control her own excitement. The world flooded with vibrant colour.

'I can't wait to see the girls' reaction. And you must ring Susan tonight,'

'Susan doesn't know,' Peter said in barely a whisper. 'I didn't want to spoil…'

Ellie nodded.

When Carolyn, waiting at home, heard the news, she began to sob, and held her father, not wanting to let go, but anxious to ring and tell Brian immediately. She was tempted to take Oliver out of school to tell him that Pa wasn't sick any more. But for all Oliver knew, Peter's sickness was a cold that wouldn't go away.

Ellie rang Claire at work, the first of many calls that afternoon. Claire said she'd come straight away, but with a signal from Peter, it was suggested she come at the usual time for a special family dinner.

'How's he coping?' she asked Ellie.

'I don't think he understands it yet,' Ellie answered.'

'Hardly surprising.'

'Sorry, darling.' Ellie in her exuberance realised she wasn't being attentive to Peter. 'I'm sorry. This is more about you than me, and I've been rattling on as if it's all about me. I can see you're tired. I know it's a shock, but the best possible kind.'

'Don't apologise, El, but I might have a rest.'

'Yes, you must.' Ellie could see his need to be alone, to take stock.

He went to the bedroom and lay down, feeling strangely ambivalent. The news had come as a great relief, an extraordinary blessing, yet even it was laced with an unease, a dislocation in the scheme of things.

The very passage of his recent life had been geared to a very particular set of eventualities. He had finally accepted them, built a protective armour around himself, and they had been snatched away. It was like having to learn how to walk again. There was a sense in which some natural law had been overridden.

The family was there for the celebratory dinner that night, though Ellie later admitted it would have been better to wait a day or two. But Peter was grateful. He needed them to be there, though he was in an emotional no man's land.

'I'm sorry, girls,' he said quietly to his daughters later that night as the family celebration was coming to an end, as if there was something fraudulent in his survival. 'You must think I'm not as thrilled as I should be. The truth is I'm not sure what I feel. I'm not sure what I should feel. Shock…yes, but I think it's more a feeling of awe. I keep asking myself why, looking for a reason. I know I'll be feeling very different tomorrow.'

Peter

Peter was right. He was feeling different the following day, and gradually settled into an even contentment. He never experienced the elation that had been his family's initial reaction, but was forever grateful and in awe. 'Humbled,' he called it.

Something of his mood was infectious. Ellie and the girls were sometimes quiet, reflective. They felt something mysterious had happened, something beyond their understanding. Beyond anyone's understanding.

'What are you thinking, Mummy?' Oliver would ask. 'Is nanna thinking what you are?'

At other times, they would be seen smiling for no apparent reason.

Peter rang Susan but decided to keep the news of his diagnosis and remarkable recovery till he could see her. He wondered if she'd be disappointed that he'd only contacted her because he thought he was dying.

A week later, as life had settled into its near-normal routines, Ellie had a heart attack in the kitchen. Claire had already gone to work. Peter was upstairs in the bedroom and heard a thump and the clatter of several pans falling to the floor.

His first reaction was to think that something had been knocked over, but when he didn't get an answer to his calls, he was alarmed and rushed downstairs to find Ellie on the floor, lying on her side, trying to prop herself into a sitting position against the fridge, and clutching at her chest. She was blanched and in terrible pain.

He rushed to the phone, rang 000, stammered an emotional plea, and sat with her on the kitchen floor with her head in his lap, stroking her moist forehead, brushing the hair from her face and telling her everything would be all right, until the ambulance came. He'd never forget her startled eyes watching him.

'Did she say anything to you, Dad…when you were waiting…and she was lying on the floor?' Carolyn, the eternal romantic asked years later hoping that sentiment had still been alive between them.

Peter couldn't remember. 'I don't think so,' he answered. 'She was in such pain, I don't think she could.'

He was allowed to ride with her in the ambulance, and it only took several minutes to arrive at the hospital. She lapsed in and out of consciousness on the way as the paramedics treated her and phoned the hospital to be ready for her arrival.

Peter didn't know much about heart attacks, but he could tell from the paramedic's urgent activity that it was serious. Their voices were hushed. He couldn't hear what they were saying. The language was technical. He felt helpless. The siren was blaring. Even with the pain, Ellie managed a weak smile for him, and squeezed his hand.

'We'll see it through together,' he said gently when she was wheeled at a frantic pace into the hospital, ever mindful that it was the message she had so often given him. There was a fainter squeeze of his hand and her eyes closed.

She was given priority in emergency and rushed to a private room, where she was examined by two doctors and attached to a number of monitors.

Peter sat stunned in the emergency waiting room with an elderly woman who was being comforted by her daughter and moaning loudly, and with a man in overalls whose arm was wrapped in a bloody towel. In moments of silence, he could hear ticking, and thought of the old man's stick tapping the floor as he left Enright's waiting room. Is time of the essence now, he wondered. It's only a clock, he told himself, but it was unnerving, ominous.

How long before I know something, he kept thinking, and asked at the reception counter only to be politely turned away, with the inevitable answer.

'The doctors will see you, Mr Allthorpe, as soon as they have something to tell you.'

After what seemed like an eternity, a middle-aged doctor with a handsome horsey face greeted him with a barely audible voice, and ushered him into a small annex away from the emergency waiting room. He didn't give a name. 'It's not too good,' he told Peter in a very businesslike way. 'We could be wrong but significant damage may have been done. We're waiting for further test results. But she's resting comfortably and being closely monitored. We're doing all we can. If there is any change, we'll let you know.'

'Thank you,' Peter mumbled. 'Can I see her?' he asked, numbed, beyond pain, and was surprised when the doctor consented. Only later would he realise why the doctor had agreed.

Minutes later, he sat bedside in her room, reassuring her as she had been doing for him for months. Her eyes were open and seemed to be reading his face. She couldn't speak but he knew she understood. Eventually her eyes closed. She lapsed into a coma.

It must have been hours later that the doctor entered the room carrying a sheaf of test results. His face was a mask. 'You need to prepare yourself, Mr Allthorpe,' he said more sympathetically. 'As I said before, there's been significant damage. I'm afraid there's not a great deal more we can do, but if there's anything you need to ask…'

'What do you mean there's nothing you can do?' Peter asked, feeling sick. 'Will she get better?'

'I can't answer that. The body is quite remarkable,' the doctor said gravely, 'but the damage…'

For the rest of the day, Peter was in a daze, sitting bedside or occasionally walking the corridors for a coffee break. He dared not leave her for more than a few minutes.

He rang the girls, who said they'd come immediately. The situation was difficult to grasp and, in his confused frame of mind, he kept entertaining the idea that one of them had been chosen and, because he'd been spared, because he'd cheated death, it had to be Ellie.

What did prepare yourself mean, he asked himself. Surely there was only one thing it could mean. He found himself mulling over a semantic analysis. 'You need to.' Not 'you might', or 'perhaps you could consider'. 'Need' carried an urgency, a finality.

They say the comatose can hear your every word as they near the end. Nurses tell you to profess your love, seek absolution, tell them you'll be fine or, if you're so inclined, pray.

And so Peter spoke to Ellie, recalling the good times, saying how lucky he was to have her, telling her that he still needed her and not to go anywhere. Sometimes he was light-hearted and laughed. At other times, he was anguished, his tears flowing like hers had secretly for him when she'd found herself alone. Occasionally, he'd lean over and kiss her forehead, avoiding the breathing equipment.

He thought of them sitting together at West Head a month ago, the warmth and stillness, the rustling of trees and smell of eucalyptus, the blueness of the sky, the bird life and lizards, the postcard panorama of the water below. And he thought of the halcyon days at Church Point wading in the warm green shallows.

The girls arrived together, and he gave them time alone with Ellie. Both were crying.

'Will she be all right, Dad?' Carolyn asked when they came out of her room, obviously shaken. 'I hope she knew we were there. Her eyes were closed. What exactly did the doctor say?'

'Are you all right?' Claire asked, and patted his shoulder.

They left well into the night, and only when he assured them that there was little they could do and that he would not leave her bedside. Perhaps they could return early in the morning.

'She might be able to talk to you then,' he whispered.

The nursing staff brought him a cup of tea and a couple of biscuits, telling him the cafeteria would be closed. They made him a makeshift couch in her room so that they could spend the night together.

There was a pervasive silence, broken only by Ellie's heavy breathing. Shadows flickered beyond the window, but he could see no moon or stars in the sky. It seemed heavy with dread, the colour of charcoal velvet. A few outdoor lights shone feebly from the hospital walls. He'd watch her face, her mouth unhinged, and listen to her stertorous breath rasp life from laden air.

His endless chatter to her revived odd images, her raiding the box of Turkish Delight and strenuously denying it, laughing as she did so, the way she'd bite her lip when curious or absorbed, her gambolling about when excited, the hilarious posturing when she addressed a drive from the tee in golf, and most of all the endless tokens and novel ways she'd come up with of showing her love.

At two thirty a.m., the grating sound stopped, and a palpable stillness filled the room. For a few seconds, Peter wondered if Ellie was enjoying a more comfortable sleep, but he soon realised the terrible truth.

Whenever people later spoke of the spirit moving, this was the moment he'd remember. He felt a sense of something passing, some essence moving from her and travelling away. There was no need to press buzzers or call for help. There was no hurry. For years, he'd try to recall the exact nature of his feelings at that moment. There was shock. It was so sudden. She'd been preparing meals in the kitchen only eighteen hours before, and with the numbness there was a profound emptiness. For months, many different feelings would jostle for the right to plead.

She was at peace now, and he didn't want to leave her. These were precious moments as she prepared for a final journey. He was a jealous lover, resentful of being disturbed, not wanting the intrusion of an indifferent world. Not yet.

It must have been two hours later that he kissed her one final time, and after lingering at the door, still reluctant to leave, approached the nurses' station to interrupt the chatter of the two night-duty nurses. He didn't say a word. One look and they knew.

One of them went to Ellie to confirm, and returned to nod. They very gently explained the procedure the hospital would follow for Ellie's release, and one of them escorted him to the front doors, placing a hand on his arm as a gesture of sympathy. He was grateful she didn't speak. Platitudes would have been hard to bear.

The car park was almost deserted as he struggled through a swirling mist. The coal sky weighed too much. He would ring the girls and Susan in the morning. It was nearly light anyway. A couple of hours would make no difference now, though they'd be crushed they hadn't been there at the end. He'd encouraged them to go home, not believing the end would come so soon.

His drive away was metaphor, consigning present loss to mellow past, advancing by retreat. The world was still asleep, the darkness blushed by amber lights threading gleaming sutures across the road, and Ellie was everywhere, the brief ubiquity that's granted when you kiss the cheek of time.

'Don't leave me,' he said aloud as he drove. 'Not yet.'

As the car moved noiselessly on empty roads, their dialogue was loving and pure, and while he was sore at heart, there were moments of strange peace. He wasn't raging against the dying of the light.

Claire and Peter

Those first weeks and months were almost unbearable. We all relied on Mum, each in our own way. She was always there for us all. Always putting us first.

To say that Dad was shattered would be an understatement. Of course he was in terrible pain, but I know he was determined to be there for Carolyn and me, just as I know he was set on being there for us because he knew it was what Mum would have wanted.

Carolyn and Brian would often come to dinner as support for us, though I know they needed the support as much as we did. Dad would make a real effort to ask about each of us. He'd even find time to play with Oliver, but shortly after we'd eaten, he'd excuse himself and go to the study to be alone. We knew not to disturb him. A couple of times when the others had gone home, I'd go and stand outside the study door. But I never heard a sound. No rustling of a turned page or shifting of a chair.

He'd often throw himself into work around the house and refuse to stop even though there was no urgency to do it. Then I'd often catch him in the garden, hands in his pockets, standing and looking down at one of the plots where Mum had planted flowers or grown vegetables.

But sometimes his behaviour was surprising. It was strange because even at that very difficult time, when he must have been hurting so much, he seemed to be experiencing moments of joy that would come suddenly like a butterfly landing on his shoulder, and I knew it had everything to do with Mum.

I never asked but I think something happened between them as Dad sat with her in the hospital. I know she couldn't speak, and wasn't even conscious, but I wonder if that matters when meaning can be passed on in so many different ways.

Carolyn was devastated but we all helped there. Brian was a tower of strength. I'd have to say the family was impressive in how it worked together, with each of us making allowances for the others, Dad with his different moods and silent retreats, Carolyn with her emotional outbursts, Oliver with his crying and constant questions, and me, well, I'm not sure what allowances were made for me. But everyone was understanding.

Pregnancy was the turning point for Carolyn. It was a surprise because it wasn't planned, and a doctor had told her not to expect any more children. But as the months passed, the new arrival absorbed her thoughts, so much so that Oliver wasn't the centre of attention and was getting a little hard to handle. She was delighted when she told us she'd called the little girl Ellie, believing she was keeping Mum's memory alive.

Dad was in regular contact with Susan. I didn't know he hadn't told her about his illness when he made that first visit. She came to stay for a few days in that first month, and that's when he told her. We all thought she was wonderful, like a female version of Dad. She became a regular visitor and a welcome addition to the family.

And he told me all about the night Susan left all those years ago, the reason they hadn't contacted each other. That poor boy. I don't think I've ever felt so close to him as when he told me the story, except perhaps for the time we took Susan to the park at Bobbin Head, and I saw the back view of the two of them sitting pressed together on a wooden bench holding hands and laughing like two little kids. He'd only recently told me about that terrible night, and all I could see or imagine was the twelve-year-old brother with his fifteen-year-old sister sitting together hand in hand, talking excitedly and scuffing the ground with their swinging feet.

I'd never left home, and I remained in the house with Dad. I had my work, and was doing well, getting a lot of recognition. I developed a strong interest in genealogy, and would spend nights on the internet. I still do. I wonder if at first it was a need to understand more about Mum and Dad, and my own place in the scheme of things.

I didn't exactly take over Mum's role, that would have been too big an expectation, but Dad and I settled into a comfortable working routine.

As the years go by, the past is supposed to become more generic than particular, truth and fiction are meant to blur, but I remember it all.

*

I've just turned ninety-three, and it's twenty-five years ago that I lost Ellie. If you think saying that is not very uplifting, you'd be wrong. Of course I miss Ellie. Not a day goes by when I don't talk with her, or give silent thanks for the many wonderful years we shared together.

I tell her what the young ones are wearing these days. I tell her of little Ellie and how she looks a lot like her, and I used to tell her of the many wonderful sharing times I had with Susan until she passed on a few years back. It might sound corny, the pabulum of the cheap magazines in Enright and Chang's waiting rooms, but in a very real sense our love lives on.

If you think such a sequence of events must also call into question the place of God or a much bigger picture of the meaning of the universe in my life, you'd be wrong again. Why should a larger meaning or a divine purpose conform to our own minuscule view?

I clung to life all those years ago. Now death has no sting. Surely all of life is a preparation for death. If well lived, if we live it in and for others, perhaps we have no right to resent having to leave it. I accept my part in the cycle of life and death, the grand plan, and am grateful for it.

The cancer, if that's what it was, never returned, and except for a few arthritic pains, I'm as well as anyone of my age could reasonably expect. Claire still lives with me, and we have a border collie, Mellow, that we spoil rotten.

We do our best to help each other in any way we can. I look after the money matters, do some of the domestic chores, and have developed an interest in growing vegetables. If only Ellie could see me now.

I did write that history of the local area, but never auditioned for a part in the Noel Coward play. I'm grateful for having sufficient mobility to walk around the supermarket once a week. It has become an important outing, releasing me from a regime of reading and work at home, to rub shoulders with the real world.

There's rarely a time I don't hear a couple of women, typically in their fifties, lamenting the onslaught of age, talking of the pigment marks on their legs, the arthritis, the way some of the body drops or sags, and sharing the ricocheting stories of early bereavements.

I just smile.